"I would have done whatever you wanted of me, Nina."

A weight lifted off her heart. On the other hand, Jack's response was entirely concentrated on her, which left out the baby.

"I don't want to live with every bit of joy being whittled away by your resentment of the baby, Jack."

He raised a hand in solemn fervor. "Nina, I swear to you I can accommodate the kid."

Nina gritted her teeth. *Accommodate the kid!* How dared he talk about Charlotte like that? It was hopeless. She picked up a strawberry and bit the fruit off its stalk, seething through its juice. Jack Gulliver might be the sexiest man alive, but he wasn't worth a father's bootlace.

EMMA DARCY nearly became an actress until her fiancé declared he preferred to attend the theater *with* her. She became a wife and mother. Later she took up oil painting—unsuccessfully, she remarks. Then she tried architecture, designing the family home in New South Wales, Australia. Next came romance writing—"the hardest and most challenging of all the activities," she confesses.

Books by Emma Darcy

HARLEQUIN PRESENTS

1745—THE FATHERHOOD AFFAIR
1771—CLIMAX OF PASSION
1785—LAST STOP MARRIAGE
1815—MISCHIEF AND MARRIAGE
1833—THE FATHER OF HER CHILD
1848—THEIR WEDDING DAY

EMMA DARCY

Jack's Baby

JACK'S BABY

Harlequin Books

TORONTO • NEW YORK • LONDON
AMSTERDAM • PARIS • SYDNEY • HAMBURG
STOCKHOLM • ATHENS • TOKYO • MILAN
MADRID • WARSAW • BUDAPEST • AUCKLAND

ISBN 0-373-11857-0

JACK'S BABY

First North American Publication 1997.

Copyright © 1997 by Emma Darcy.

This edition published by arrangement with Harlequin Books S.A.

® and TM are trademarks of the publisher. Trademarks indicated with
® are registered in the United States Patent and Trademark Office, the
Canadian Trade Marks Office and in other countries.

Printed in U.S.A.

CHAPTER ONE

BABIES, Jack Gulliver darkly reflected, under-mined every normal, congenial intercourse be-tween intelligent adults. They infiltrated people's lives even before they entered the world, then took over like tyrannical dictators. Nothing was safe from them.

Jack brooded over these truths as he drove through the tunnel under Sydney Harbour, taking the shortest route to Paddington and the Royal Hospital for Women. He wished Maurice had been satisfied with hearty congratulations on the birth of his son. It was totally unreasonable of him to insist Jack actually come and view the new pride and joy. Paternal enthusiasm run rampant. Jack wondered how long it would last.

One by one his friends had succumbed to the lure of fatherhood, only to find themselves knocked off their happy perches of being the main focus of attention in their households. They'd groaned out their misery and their com-plaints to him, envying his freedom from the chaos they had brought upon themselves.

"Good sex is impossible."

"You're lucky if you get any sex."

"Who wants sex? I'd like one—just one—full night's sleep."

"Forget spontaneity. The baby comes first, first, first and first."

"I haven't got a wife. She's turned into a slave to the baby."

"There's no time for *us* any more."

"It's like moving an army to go anywhere. I'd rather stay at home. Save the aggravation."

There was no doubt in Jack's mind that babies were destructive little monsters. They probably should be born with a 007 warning engraved on their foreheads—licenced to kill. He knew of several couples who had broken up under the stress of parenthood, and the rest were struggling to adjust to changes they resented.

Jack now had a fair appreciation of why his own parents had limited their progeny to one only, why he had been brought up by nannies and shunted off to boarding school at age seven. Quite clearly he had interfered too much with their lives. From his current view as an adult, he understood they had taken practical steps to minimise the damage to their rights as individuals, but as a child, Jack hadn't liked being on the receiving end of their solutions.

The lonely, shut-out feeling of his youth was still an unhappy memory. No way would he inflict the same process on a child of his. On the other hand, he was quite sure he wouldn't like such a disruptive influence in his life, either. The solution, as he saw it, was simple. Don't have children.

Any curiosity he might have had about the experience of fatherhood had been more than fulfilled by what he'd observed with his friends. Apart from which, he felt no urge to perpetuate his bloodline. He enjoyed his life, loved his work, had the financial freedom to do what he liked when he liked. What more could he want?

Nina...

Jack grimaced as he tried to expunge that thought and the gut-wrenching sense of loss accompanying it. Nina had shut him out even more thoroughly than his parents had, not even giving him the chance to open the door again. All over a stupid argument about babies.

Or maybe there'd been other reasons. He shook his head, still frustrated by the way she'd cut him out of her life, leaving him wondering what he'd done wrong. He'd chosen that very night to ask Nina to move in with him, sure in his own mind he'd found a woman he'd enjoy living with, and just because he'd made a few entirely appropriate comments about the baby who'd wrecked the dinner party they'd attended, Nina had gone off her brain and dumped him, then and there. No comeback. Total wipe-out.

It made no sense to him. He was probably well rid of a woman who could act so irrationally. Yet there'd never been a glimmer of such behaviour in all the time they'd spent together—months of sheer joy. He could have sworn they were completely compatible, even to their pleasure in the creative work they did. She was the first and only person he'd ever felt really at home with.

There were times he missed her so badly it was a physical ache. He could still visualise her as clearly as if she were with him now, sitting beside him—dark velvet eyes with stars in them, a smile that made his heart dance, shiny black hair swinging around her shoulders, her soft, feminine curves a sensual promise he knew to be absolutely true. He could hear her infectious laughter and the sexy murmurs that excited him when they made love.

Futile memories. He wished he could forget Nina Brady and how he'd felt with her. There was no shortage of women wanting to interest him. Sooner or later he'd meet one who'd strike that special spark. It was only a matter of waiting. Eight months hardly rated as a long time. In a year or two, Nina's rejection wouldn't mean a thing.

The traffic lights favoured him right up to Taylor Square. As he turned into Oxford Street, he switched his mind to Maurice and tried to work himself into a lighter mood. Maurice Larosa was a good friend and a valuable business associate. He not only gave Jack all the French polishing work on the antiques he sold, but frequently sent clients who wanted to have pieces made to match furniture they'd bought. Favours like that deserved favours in return, and if it meant smiling benevolently at a baby, Jack was resolved on obliging. At least this once.

He spotted a car pulling out of a convenient space and shot into it, grateful not to waste time hunting for a parking slot. The hospital was only a short distance away. The dash clock showed seven-fifteen, plenty of time to get there, perform as expected and take his leave with the excuse of giving Maurice and his wife privacy to say their good nights.

He picked up the gift-boxed bottle of champagne from the passenger seat, smiling over this particular forethought as he alighted from the big Range Rover and locked it. Other visitors would undoubtedly shower presents on the baby. Some French bubbly might give the new and soon-to-be-frazzled parents a pleasant hour or two together. He knew from his other friends that babies killed any sense of romance stone dead.

Although it was April, there wasn't so much as a nip of autumn in the air. The lingering Indian summer made it a pleasant hour for walking. A waste of a nice evening, Jack thought, as he entered the hospital and headed for the inquiries desk. Having received directions, he caught the elevator to the correct floor, mentally bracing himself to endure baby talk with jovial indulgence for a minimum of twenty minutes.

The elevator doors opened. He stepped out. Something familiar about the woman waiting to step into the compartment caught his eye. He looked sharply at her and he had the weird sense of falling down an empty shaft instead of standing flat on a firm floor.

"Nina?"

Her name exploded from his throat.

Her hair was cropped short, but he couldn't mistake that face, those eyes as she stared straight at him. Recognition, shock, disbelief, fear, anger...each expression pulsed briefly at him from a stillness that shrieked with tension. Then she whirled past him, jabbed a finger at the control panel inside the elevator and hugged herself against the back wall, glaring a fierce rejection of him until the doors closed.

The message burned into his brain. She didn't want him. She didn't want anything to do with him. He quelled the raging instinct to chase after her, find her, make her listen to him. Useless. She'd made her decision to shut him out. It hadn't changed. It wasn't about to change. She'd just done it again.

He forced himself to walk away, to check the room numbers he passed along the corridor. He'd come here to oblige a friend. Never mind that he had no heart for it. It gave him something purposeful to do. He had to forget Nina.

But why had there been fear in her eyes? He'd never given her any reason to be afraid of him.

Why anger? Surely she realised this meeting was purely accidental.

Damn it all! What had he done wrong?

CHAPTER TWO

JACK...

His name kept pounding through Nina's mind, creating waves of pain that seemed to suck at her body, leaving her weak and trembling. When the elevator doors opened, she had to push herself away from the wall. Her legs were like jelly, her stomach a churning mess. Somehow she made it to the ladies' rest room on the ground floor, blundered into an empty cubicle, fastened the door, then gratefully sank onto the toilet seat, safely hidden until she could pull herself together.

Tears welled into her eyes. She hunched over, burying her face in her hands, rocking in anguish at the unkind stroke of fate that had brought her face to face with Jack at such a time and place. It wasn't fair. It was grossly unfair. She'd spent the past eight months trying to forget him, forcing herself to accept there could be no happy future with him. Seeing him again now opened up all the hurt she'd done her best to bury.

For one heart-stopping moment she'd thought he knew. But he couldn't. And, of course, he didn't. The surprise on his face told her he hadn't expected to run into her.

The husky urgency in his voice had rattled memories better suppressed. Jack wanting her, making love to her with such intense passion they seemed to flow together in a fusing heat that had made her feel it was impossible to tear them apart. They'd been a perfect match in so many ways…if there were only two of them. She hadn't known then, hadn't realised there was a fatal flaw in their relationship, silently waiting to explode in her face, just when she'd fooled herself everything would be all right.

The hollow sickness she had felt that night swamped her again. Jack was lost to her. Irrevocably. Their paths had diverged so deeply, no meeting place was left for them. An unpredictable and accidental crossing like tonight was a cruelty, a glimpse of what might have been if Jack's attitude about babies and having children had been different.

Nina remembered her own father's attitude too well to inflict the same crushing sense of being unwanted onto any child, much less her own. Every time her parents had argued, they had invariably flung out the bitter accusation of being trapped by an unplanned pregnancy. Nina was to blame for her father not being in the career he wanted, for her mother being tied to responsibility instead of enjoying many more carefree years. The list of resentments was endless.

It would have been the same with Jack—different reasons for resenting the situation but no difference in the feelings aroused. He had left her with no doubt about that. Nina shut her eyes tight, squeezing back the futile tears, wishing she could erase the image of him, stamped so freshly on her mind.

He was still magnetically handsome, emanating the same powerful virility that had drawn her to him at their very first meeting. In just those few strung-out moments before she'd escaped via the elevator, the old familiarities had leapt to vivid life again—the small mole near his jawline, a tantalising little disfigurement on his smoothly tanned skin. His streaky toffee hair, at its shaggy state, needing a trim. The startling directness of his green eyes tugging at her heart.

He shouldn't affect her like this. Not now, when it was so impossibly hopeless for them ever to get together. And this was the last place he should be. Why on earth would Jack be visiting a maternity hospital?

Someone must have pressed him to come, blindly intent on showing off a new son or daughter, not realising a baby had no appeal whatsoever to Jack Gulliver. Social politeness or professional sensibilities would have pushed him to oblige. It was the only answer Nina could come up with. She desperately hoped that seeing her wouldn't prompt a curiosity to know why she was here. If he found out...

She couldn't bear it. She just couldn't bear it. Arguments, recriminations, an insistence on shouldering some responsibility, financial if nothing else. Trapped by a child he didn't want but felt obliged to support. A tie between them going on and on...the bitterness of it. She'd hate it. She'd taken every step she could to avoid it— leaving her job, changing house, no telephone number in her name—all to make the break from Jack a completely clean one.

She wanted to howl out her fear and frustration, but if someone heard her it would draw unwelcome attention. A nurse might be fetched. Her chest hurt. Her throat ached. She grabbed some toilet tissue and mopped her eyes and cheeks, determined to rise above this dreadful stress.

Yet if the decisions she had put into action were sabotaged now, how would she cope? Her emotional state was shockingly fragile as it was, without Jack intruding on the life she had to establish and maintain. With Sally's help she could manage. She didn't need Jack's money, and her child certainly didn't need his attitude.

Maybe she was worrying for nothing. Jack's surprise didn't necessarily mean he was still interested in her. He could be attached to some other woman by now. There would have been plenty wanting to interest him in the past eight months. A good-looking man of substance didn't go begging for female company.

But what they had shared had been special. And Jack was choosy. He didn't give out to many people. The look in his eyes after the initial shock of recognition—eagerness, hope—would he shrug it off and let it go?

With any luck he might have assumed she was another visitor, passing through, leaving as he was arriving. Had he noticed she wasn't wearing proper clothes? She groaned as she realised it was more than clothes adding up the evidence against being a visitor. No make-up, hair in disarray, no handbag. She hoped she hadn't given him enough time to register those details.

Time... She glanced at her watch. Seven thirty-six. She couldn't risk running into Jack again. Best to stay hidden in this rest room until after the eight o'clock curfew for visitors. Sally would stay with the baby until she returned to the ward. There was no cause for panic. Sally expected her to spend twenty minutes or so browsing through the magazines available at the kiosk. Nina had left her happily chatting to the other two new mothers and their visitors—husbands, happy husbands and fathers.

The tears welled again. It was miserable being a single mother when she was faced with families celebrating their new offspring. Sally was a great friend and wonderful support, but it wasn't the same.

If only Jack...

Damn him! Why couldn't he have been different? Why were children so wrong for him?

CHAPTER THREE

SMILING benevolently did not come easily. Jack had to work hard at repressing the angry frustration that seeing Nina had stirred. He wanted to snap and snarl. He felt a deep empathy with his dog's behaviour when a great bone was moved out of his marked territory. He felt no empathy whatsoever with the drivel coming out of Maurice's mouth.

"He's got my ears, poor little blighter."

Jack smiled. "Well, one can always resort to plastic surgery."

Maurice laughed indulgently. "They're not that bad. He'll grow into them."

"Bound to," Jack agreed, his face aching with smiling.

Maurice looked besottedly at his wife. "I'm glad he's got Ingrid's nose."

Jack obediently performed the comparison, studying the straight, aristocratic nose of Maurice's buxom blonde wife and the longer, slightly bumpy one of his friend. He forced another smile. "Yes. Much the better nose."

Why was it obligatory to divide a baby's features between the parents? It was inevitably done, like a ritual, perhaps affirming true heritage, or an assurance that a little replica would fulfil its parents' expectations. Not only was it a deadly boring exercise to Jack, it almost drove him to snap, "Let the kid be himself, for God's sake!"

But that wasn't the done thing.

He wondered whom Nina had been visiting on this floor. Not that it mattered. No point in trying to find some contact point with her. From the attitude she had flashed to him, it would probably constitute harassment. Besides, Jack had a built-in inhibitor against going where he wasn't wanted.

"Give me the baby, darling, while you open Jack's present," Ingrid commanded, brandishing the newborn power of being a mother. This was definitely one time she could boss Maurice around. The proud and grateful Dad would undoubtedly lick her feet if she asked him to. Jack knew from observation that the flow of uncritical giving wouldn't last.

He watched Maurice lay the precious bundle in his wife's arms with tender care. It was really a pity such blissful harmony didn't last. They looked good—loving mother and father with child. Idyllic. The rot didn't set in until they went home from hospital.

Ingrid's long blonde hair gleamed like skeins of silk falling over her shoulders. Jack frowned at the reminder of Nina's hair, which some idiot had clearly butchered. What had possessed her to have her beautiful hair cut? She'd looked like a ragamuffin, wispy bits sticking out as though she'd run her fingers through the short crop instead of brushing it. The style didn't suit her. It made her face look thinner.

Maybe her face *was* thinner.

Had Nina been ill?

It was a disturbing thought. Frustration boiled up again. He hated not knowing what had been happening to her. Her face had looked paler than he remembered, too, all healthy colour washed out of it. If she'd been ill, was ill...no, it still made no sense for Nina to look at him with fear and anger.

It was no reason to cut him out of her life, either. She could have stayed with him. He would have looked after her. Did she have anyone looking after her now?

"My favourite champagne, Veuve Cliquot!" Maurice beamed at him. "Great gift, Jack."

"I won't be able to drink it," Ingrid wailed. "It'll sour my milk."

New regime rolling in, souring more than her milk, Jack silently predicted. He grimaced an apology. "Sorry, Ingrid. I'm an ignorant male."

"Never mind, love." Maurice dropped a kiss on her puckered forehead. "We'll keep it until the little guzzler here goes onto a bottle."

"I don't know when that will be." She pouted. "Look how big my breasts are swelling up with milk. They're even beginning to leak."

They were certainly stretching her nightgown to its limits of stretchability, Jack observed, and suddenly had a flash of Nina in the elevator, her arms hugging her rib cage, her breasts pushed up, surely far more voluptuous than they used to be.

She'd been wearing a loose, button-through dress, her shape disguised by it initially. Besides, his attention had been riveted on her face then, the expression in her eyes. But when she'd turned around in the elevator, pressing back against the wall, holding herself defensively, her breasts had definitely bulged.

His heart skittered. He gave himself a mental shake, pushing the idea away. To associate Nina's breasts with Ingrid's—swollen with milk—was a neurotic vision he could well do without. Nina couldn't have had a baby. It was only eight months since she'd left him.

After an argument about babies.

His mind whirled at sickening speed. Maternity hospital... not a dress, a free-flowing housecoat... tired, careless of her appearance... shock, disbelief, fear at seeing him here... anger...

He felt the blood draining from his face. He clenched his hands, gritted his teeth and willed his heart to pump his circulation back into top working order. He had to think clearly and rationally, not leap to wild conclusions. If Nina had been pregnant, surely to God she would have told him. Flung it in his face, most likely, in the middle of that argument. She couldn't have thought he'd turn his back on her.

Maybe she had thought it, deciding to take that initiative herself rather than confront what he might say or do, given his negative attitude to having children.

Nausea cramped his stomach and shot bile up his throat. If she'd gone it alone because she hadn't trusted him to respond supportively...

"Are you all right, Jack?"

Maurice's question broke through the glaze of horror in his mind. They were looking quizzically at him. Had he missed something? *Apart from a nine-month pregnancy?*

"Sorry." He sucked in a deep breath and swallowed hard. "I was just thinking how great the three of you look together."

Ingrid laughed. "Time you found yourself a wife and started a family, Jack."

Join the club. They all said that. Once they were caught in the family trap, it was as though anyone who was free of it was an offensive reminder of what they'd given up. The hell of it was he might very well have a child somewhere on this ward, a child whose mother had decided was better off fatherless than having Jack in their lives.

"Aren't you thirty-something?" Ingrid persisted.

"Darling, I'm forty," Maurice reminded her. "Age has nothing to do with it. If I hadn't met you, I'd still be a freewheeling bachelor like Jack."

Jack didn't want to be a freewheeling bachelor. He wanted Nina. He didn't care if she came with a child. He wanted Nina. The need and desire for her burgeoned out of the emptiness that had haunted the past eight months, growing with compelling force, overpowering all his objections to babies.

A little scrap of humanity like the one in Ingrid's arms couldn't beat him. He'd learn how to handle the child. He'd never had a problem handling anything once he set his mind to it. If Nina needed proof of that, he'd give it to her.

Babies were probably only destructive monsters because parents allowed them to take over. Jack was made of sterner stuff. Having seen the damage babies wrought on relationships, he could take protective steps and save Nina and himself a lot of unnecessary stress. It was all a matter of attitude and organisation.

What he needed was a plan.

He also needed definite facts instead of suppositions. A plan could very quickly come unstuck if he didn't have his facts right. Therefore, step one was to grab a nurse and make a few pertinent inquiries.

"You know, Jack—" Ingrid eyed him speculatively "—I have a few girlfriends you might enjoy meeting."

The good old matchmaking trick.

Jack smiled. He didn't even have to force it. His heart had lifted with a swelling sense of purpose. "Actually, Ingrid, I'm on my way to meet a lady I'm very interested in. If you and Maurice will excuse me... It's a delight to see you so happy, and I hope the new son and heir thrives as he should under your loving care. He's sure to be a great kid.''

Pleasure all around.

Having delivered his benevolent performance, Jack was well-wished on his way. In truth, he *was* feeling benevolent towards Maurice and Ingrid. Even their baby. They'd done him a great favour. If it wasn't for them he wouldn't have come here, wouldn't have seen Nina and put two and two together.

Only in this case, two and two were going to make three. Jack had no compunction about changing the mathematics of the situation. He was determined on being counted *in*, not *out*.

CHAPTER FOUR

VISITING hours had ended ten minutes ago. Nevertheless, Nina apprehensively checked the ward corridor, glancing swiftly to both right and left, confirming an all clear before scooting out of the elevator. It was only fifteen metres to her room. She covered the distance as fast as she could without actually running. Hearing Sally's cheerful voice still rattling away was an assurance that everything was normal.

No-one called out her name. Jack didn't suddenly emerge from one of the rooms in front of her. She reached her door, and with a thundering sense of being home free swung into the room and quickly closed the door behind her, safeguarding against a casual glance inside from any passer-by.

"There you are," Sally said with satisfaction. "I was about to send out a search party."

"Sorry." Nina turned to her friend, flashing an appeasing smile, and the world tilted as Jack filled her vision, Jack cradling her baby in the crook of his arm. She feebly fumbled for the door, instinctively seeking support, feeling herself sway alarmingly.

"Are you okay?" Anxious question from Sally.

"Here! Quick!" Jack, commanding.

Double vision. Two Jacks bundling babies into two Sallys' arms, furniture wavering all over the place. Nina closed her eyes. Too difficult to get things straight. Hopelessly dizzy.

Strong arms hooking around her, scooping her off her feet, carrying her, sitting her on the side of the bed, holding her safe, thrusting her head down. "Deep breaths, Nina. Sally, put the kid in its bassinette and pour Nina a glass of water."

The kid.

A murderous haze billowed into Nina's fuzzy mind. Her baby—the baby who'd grown inside her for nine long, miserable, lonely months— dismissed as a kid! If she had the strength, she'd put her hands around Jack's neck and strangle him. How dared he come in here, after all he'd said, and actually hold the child he didn't want, pretending he didn't mind?

The kid. Not the baby. Not our daughter. The kid. That said it all to Nina. He probably hadn't even asked what sex the baby was. Didn't care. Her heart pumped with furious vigour, clearing her head so fast she didn't need the glass of water Sally pressed into her hand.

She was tempted to hurl it in Jack's face. It might sober him up. Whatever impulsive and stupid ardour had driven him into this room needed dampening down. He wasn't thinking straight, any more than she'd been seeing straight. But she could see straight through him! Having figured out what she was doing in a maternity ward, he had a hot case of guilt.

"You need looking after, Nina," he said gruffly. "And I'm the man to do it. Drink up now."

She sipped, just to moisten her throat. Then she glared her outrage at him. "Don't you tell me what to do, Jack Gulliver. You have no right."

He returned a determined look. "I contributed to this situation and—"

"You did not." She cut him off with more belligerent determination. "You trusted me to get the contraception right, and I messed up. It's all my fault."

"Accidents happen," he said grimly.

"Well, you don't have to pay for this one. I take full responsibility."

"Sure! And you're doing a fine job of it, letting yourself get so run down you almost faint at the sight of me."

"Shock. You holding a baby was more than my mind could encompass."

"Then you'd better get used to it, Nina, because that kid happens to be my kid, too."

Her teeth clenched. Her eyes sizzled him to a crisp. "She is not a kid."

"You're right," he snapped. "More like a mind-bending drug than a natural member of the animal kingdom."

"Huh! Now you're showing your true colours."

"Just pointing out how distorted your judgment is." His eyes flashed green fire. "Denying me the right to know I've fathered a

child. Denying me the right to make my own decisions. Denying me any chance to stand by you
through what has obviously been a rough time.
Even a murderer gets his day in court.''

The fierce flow of accusations stunned her for
a moment. Justification sped off her tongue.
''You told me you don't want children, Jack
Gulliver. So don't come the injured party to me.
I left you free and clear.''

''I didn't say I wanted to be free and clear. I
don't,'' he retorted emphatically. ''I was just
asking your friend, Sally, how quickly a wedding
could be arranged.''

''A wedding!'' Shock rolled through her mind
again, sapping her energy. She took another sip
of water, then handed the glass to Sally, who was
still standing by, dumbstruck by the verbals
zipping back and forth. Nina gave her a hard,
warning look. ''What have you been telling him,
Sally?''

''Me?'' she squeaked. Her mobile face worked
through alarm and wary consideration and settled
on rueful resignation. ''Well, uh, he asked me
who I was and I, um, gave him my business
card.''

The card! Customised Weddings—We Deliver
Your Dream. With her address and telephone
number clearly printed on it!

Nina groaned, realizing the milk was spilled
and couldn't be put back into the bottle. She
sagged onto her pillow, swung her legs onto the
bed and turned away from them, closing her eyes,

unutterably depressed by an outcome she would have done anything to avoid.

"If I've done the wrong thing..." Sally's anxious voice floated over her.

"Don't blame Sally for letting the cat out of the bag, Nina," Jack quietly interposed. "I would have found out anyway."

That was probably true. Jack didn't let go of anything until he was satisfied. Like restoring a piece of antique furniture. He'd work at it and work at it until it was finished precisely as he wanted. Seeing her had done the damage, not Sally's blabbing.

Nina was suddenly aware of the silence in the room. The other visitors had gone. The babies were quiet. No-one had turned on a television set. Undoubtedly this little real-life drama was more interesting, the unmarried mother confronted by the father of her child. And Jack was so good-looking, so impressively steadfast in rebutting her charges. The two secure wives who shared this room would be looking with favour on him, not knowing what Nina knew.

It was sickening.

"A cup of tea," Sally said as though plucking the idea out of a tank of possible solutions to the situation. "I'll go and make one for her, Jack."

"Good idea," he approved warmly.

She heard Sally leave. The sound of a chair being shifted and the squeak of its upholstery told her Jack had sat down, settling in for a siege on her solitary position.

No point in hiding from him, Nina decided reluctantly. The music had to be faced, and it was better to get it over with here and now. She rolled onto her back, opened her eyes and steeled herself against the tug of attraction that hadn't diminished at all with either time or circumstances.

He met her gaze with direct intensity, his expression a moving mixture of compassion and resolution. Tears pricked her eyes. He cared about her. The baby was a complication he didn't want, but his feeling for her hadn't changed. It made the necessity of rejecting him again all the more difficult and painful.

It would be so easy to reach out and take the comfort and warmth and pleasure of being with him again. He'd wrap her in his arms and stroke her back and kiss her hair, and she'd feel his body stir with desire for her and ... She'd missed him so much. But if she gave in to the need aching through her now, Jack would be encouraged to stick around, and the inevitable consequences would be worse than her current sense of deprivation.

Better to remain independent.

"I don't need your help, Jack," she said flatly.

"That's not how it looks to me, Nina." He reached out and took her left hand, fondling it warmly, persuasively pressing a link between them as he added, "I think we should get married as soon as possible."

"No!" She snatched her hand away, feeling as though he'd burned her. Her eyes blazed fierce conviction. "I won't marry you, Jack."

"Why not? It's the most sensible, practical thing to do."

"I will not subject my baby to a father who doesn't want her."

"If you're worried about the kid, let me assure you—"

"Her name," Nina interrupted furiously, "is Charlotte."

"Charlotte?" He frowned. "It doesn't go very well with Gulliver. Let's toss a few other names around."

"Charlotte Brady sounds fine to me."

Jack studied the stubborn set of her face and made a political retreat. "Fine. If that's the name you like, I'm happy to go along with it." He brightened. "On second thoughts, Charlotte isn't too bad. We can call her Charlie. Charlie Gulliver has a nice ring to it."

"Charlotte is a girl, Jack," Nina pointed out with seething emphasis. "She is *my* daughter and she will remain Charlotte Brady. I am not going to marry you."

He sighed. Heavily. His eyes glittered with devious intent. "Okay. We'll just live together then."

"I have no intention of living with you, Jack. I have my own place. I have everything set up as I want it, and neither I nor my baby requires your support."

"Brave words, Nina, but what if something goes wrong with your well-laid plans?"

"I'll cope."

"You'll cope better with me at your side."

"No, I won't."

"We'll see about that," he declared, letting her know he was not about to be put off, put down or put out.

Nina sighed. Heavily. Jack was going to make a battle of it, no matter what she said. A wave of weakness dragged through her. She wished Charlotte would start bawling her head off. That would soon shift Jack. If her cries set the other babies off, too, he'd be out the door as fast as his feet could carry him.

Sally returned, darting apprehensive looks at Jack and Nina as she put the cup of tea on the mobile tray. "Better now?" she asked hopefully.

Sally Bloomfield was the most assertive person Nina had ever met. She was a brilliant saleswoman, able to talk anybody into anything and make him feel delighted about it. Her appearance was always polished and professional, from her chic auburn hair to her beautifully shod feet. Her smile dazzled, and her bright hazel eyes mesmerised. Sally sailed through life with the blissful belief that no matter what happened, it would turn out for the best. Her optimism was good to be around, but right now Nina needed her professional expertise.

"Tell Jack I'm perfectly capable of doing without him, Sally," she appealed.

"Right!" She sat herself at the end of the bed and addressed Jack gravely. "It's like this. Nina and I are set up in business together."

Jack looked surprised. "Nina is organising weddings, too?"

"No, no, that's my specialty. I adore weddings. Nina is a great seamstress. She fixes any bridal hire gowns that need altering. Does extra beading and tucks and stuff. Some of our clients have chosen Nina's own designs, and she makes them so beautifully, it adds a lot to our reputation of delivering the dream."

Jack frowned. "She won't have much time for that with the baby. They're time-consuming little mo—" He caught his breath.

"Monsters," Nina finished for him. "Go on. Say it, Jack. That's how you think of them. Monsters!"

"I was going to say moppets," he corrected her loftily.

"Huh!"

"Well, the thing is," Sally said swiftly, "Nina doesn't have to travel anywhere. Everything is very handy. The business is run from my home, and Nina has a completely self-contained granny flat at the back of the premises. She can bring the baby into the house with her when she has to do fittings. There's really no problem. She's got a solid income, good accommodation and nothing to worry about."

"You see? I'm self-sufficient," Nina declared triumphantly.

"Except for a man," Sally muttered.

Nina glared at her.

Sally shrugged and flirted with her eyes at Jack. "Well, you must admit, Nina, he is superb lover material. Why not have him? You can always get rid of a husband if it doesn't work out."

"Excellent reasoning." Jack leapt in eagerly. "If she'd just give me a chance—"

"I am not going to marry him," Nina interrupted.

"There's a lot of advantages to it, Nina," Sally argued. "Where would I be without my husbands? I got a car out of the first, a house out of the second and the capital to set up the business from the third."

Sally had it the wrong way round. Nina didn't want a sales pitch directed at her, but Sally had the bit between the teeth and was in full spate.

"Husbands can be very handy. You have a built-in escort, sex on demand, someone to look after you if you get sloshed at a party, financial backing, the muscle to stand over tradesmen and make sure they do the job right, and in your case, a no-cost baby minder when you want a break from mothering."

"That's where it falls down," Nina pounced. "Jack hates babies."

"It's different with my own kid," he defended staunchly.

Nina swung on him. "What's different about it? You think Charlotte won't cry? That she won't dirty her nappy and wake up in the middle of the night and take attention away from you?"

"I can adjust."

"Ingrained attitudes do not disappear overnight, Jack Gulliver."

A nurse came in and looked disapprovingly at the late visitors. "I'm afraid I'll have to ask you people to leave. Hospital rules, you know."

Sally hopped off the bed. "Sleep on it, Nina," she advised, her eyebrows waggling suggestively. "It's very easy to get a divorce these days."

Jack rose reluctantly from his chair. "I'll be back tomorrow, Nina," he vowed, a challenge burning in his eyes. "I'm not going to be shut out again."

Then he turned to look down at the baby in the bassinette, giving her a salute as he moved past. "Good night, kid. This is your dad talking, and don't let your mum tell you any different."

"Her name is Charlotte!" Nina shouted after him.

CHAPTER FIVE

THE roses arrived just before the midmorning feeding time. One of the nurses carried in the huge arrangement, grinning from ear to ear. "Three dozen!" she crowed, eyeing Nina with speculative interest. Being given so many was clearly a notable achievement.

"For me?" Nina asked doubtfully.

"It's your name on the envelope," came the ready assurance.

They could only be from Jack. Which meant he really would be coming back today, bringing with him all the conflicts she had tried to keep out of the life she had planned for Charlotte and herself. With her heart aflutter with apprehension and her mind clogged with a host of desires she shied away from examining, Nina cleared the top of her bedside cabinet before she was aware of what she was doing.

The nurse set the vase down just as Nina realised she should refuse the extravagant gift. It was weak to give Jack any positive signals. But the deep red buds had a glorious scent, and they were so heart-liftingly beautiful, it seemed unnecessarily churlish to direct them elsewhere. It wouldn't make any difference in the long run, she argued to herself. The roses would die, just as Jack's interest in wooing her would die when the crunch of actually having to deal with a baby came.

Having spent a restless night brooding over Jack's reappearance in her life, Nina remained unpersuaded there was any real hope of a happy future with him. All she could see ahead of them were endless disputes, damaging to everyone, especially Charlotte.

Recollections of her own childhood were still painfully vivid. Her parents had finally separated when she was ten, and she'd been shunted off to live with her grandmother, who was prepared to shoulder the burden. Despite being tolerated, rather than loved, by her grandmother, Nina had found it an enormous relief simply no longer being a bone of continual contention between her parents.

The nurse unpinned the envelope and gave it to her, still grinning. "Red roses for love. Some guy wants to make an impression."

"He already has," Nina muttered darkly, and Jack had a lot of winning over to do before she'd change her mind about his fitness to be a father. "Thanks for bringing them in."

"My pleasure."

Nina opened the envelope and withdrew the card. It read, "For the woman who's given me more than anyone else in the world—Love, Jack."

A lump filled her throat. She had to swallow hard to ease the constriction. The truth of it was

Jack had given her more than any man she had ever met, but that did not make him right for Charlotte. Clinging to the conviction he could not be trusted to love their daughter as she should be loved, Nina opened the top drawer of her cabinet and dropped the card in, denying herself the indulgence of reading it over and over again, making more of it than it meant.

"Looks like your Jack is making up for lost time."

The optimistic comment from Rhonda, one of her room-mates, struck a sensitive chord. Had she done wrong in denying Jack knowledge of her pregnancy? At the time she had imagined a horrified reaction from him. She had believed he would suggest an abortion and do his utmost to harass her into it. Maybe she had done him an injustice.

Nevertheless, the situation last night had been a very different one. A baby who was already born could not be as easily dismissed as an unseen fetus. It was a reality, a living, breathing human being, who was definitely a little person in her own right, one who couldn't be ignored or discarded as of no account.

Jack might want to diminish her importance, but no way was Nina going to let him relegate Charlotte to some distant place in their lives. Calling her the kid was so offensively impersonal. Nina still burned at the offhand attitude it typified. And corrupting their daughter's name to Charlie . . . No doubt if he had to have a child, he would have preferred a boy.

"Three dozen hothouse roses don't come cheaply," came the knowing remark from Kim, her other room-mate.

"He can afford them. It's not money that worries him," Nina said dryly, niggled by the unsubtle approbation both women had displayed towards Jack since his dramatic appearance on the scene last night. They couldn't seem to comprehend her reservations about accepting his volte-face on wanting a child in his life.

They were younger than Nina, and the course of their lives had run with conventional smoothness so far. They had every reason to cling to their romantic illusions, not having run into any serious snags themselves.

Kim, at twenty-three, was a rather plump but pretty blonde who'd married the guy she fell in love with at high school. The only career she wanted was being his wife and the mother of his children. Her husband had a permanent job on the railway, and she felt absolutely secure.

Rhonda, at twenty-five, was more sophisticated, a professional hairdresser who intended to keep working until she and her husband had their house paid off. He was a sales representative of a major food company, and their goals had been meticulously planned—their wedding, the baby, the house, their car traded in for a family station wagon.

Rhonda's catalogued milestones had driven Nina to reflect that none of her own goals had been achieved. She'd worked her way through design school, dreaming of making a name for herself in the fashion industry. Clinching an apprenticeship with a successful designer had seemed a helpful step, yet it had very quickly punched home to her that she'd never have the capital to launch her own brand name in such a highly competitive field. The closest she'd got to establishing her own business was this partnership with Sally.

As for her love-life, there had been no-one of any deep significance until Jack. She'd been twenty-eight at the time of meeting him, Jack thirty-two, and it truly seemed as though Mr. Right had finally come along. The shock had been totally shattering when he'd revealed how anti babies and children he was. Even if she hadn't been pregnant, it would have made her think twice about continuing their relationship.

Charlotte stirred, giving one of her little mewing cries. Nina swooped on the bassinette, eager to pick up her beautiful baby daughter and cradle her in her arms. She was so tiny and perfect, like a miracle, and Nina still marvelled at the way she latched instantly onto a nipple and sucked.

Having stacked the pillows on the bed for a comfortable position, Nina settled back against them, unbuttoned her nightie and smilingly watched her daughter home in on what she wanted. A rush of deep maternal love reassured Nina of the decisions she had made, despite the situation with Jack.

Although she had never felt a pressing need to have a baby, it had always seemed to her a natural thing to do somewhere along her lifeline. She would have wanted the choice to have a child and would have felt cheated as a woman to be denied it. Maybe it was some subconscious response to not having been wanted herself, but from the moment Nina had learnt she was pregnant, however unplanned it was, all her protective instincts had been aroused. This baby would be wanted and loved and cherished.

She might have been a failure as a daughter, a failure at making a name for herself with her own fashion label, a failure at picking the right man to love, but she was not going to be a failure as a mother. On that Nina was fiercely resolved.

"If your Jack doesn't worry about money he must have a great job," Rhonda remarked, obviously interested in the financial angle. She had a budget worked out for everything.

"He runs his own business," Nina explained.

"Doing what?" Kim pumped.

Nina sighed and gave in to their natural curiosity. "Mostly French polishing. He restores antiques and makes cabinets and other bits and pieces. He's very good at it."

A perfectionist, she thought. Like her with her sewing and dress designs. They both enjoyed making something beautiful. Their mutual understanding of the pleasure and satisfaction in creativity was one of the shared bonds that had made their relationship so good.

She wished she could believe in Jack's turn-around. Maybe she should risk the hurt of giving him a chance. If he persisted. The roses were a heady reminder of Jack's sensuality. A convulsive little shiver ran over her skin. She had missed the enthralling intimacy of his love-making. Sally had a point there. The nights were very lonely by herself.

"I wish my husband was a handy man," Rhonda said ruefully. "He can't even change a tap washer."

"You can always get in a plumber. You can't hire a doting and devoted father," Nina pointed out, reminding herself to be very, very wary of where she was heading with Jack, if indeed she was heading anywhere. There would inevitably be a lot of interrupted nights with Charlotte. Jack's groaning and grumbling wouldn't exactly be music to her ears.

"Give him time to feel like a father," Kim advised. "Does Charlotte favour him in looks?"

"Not particularly."

She looked at their daughter. Her fair hair probably came from him. Not that Jack was fair now, but he must have been when he was a boy. Nina remembered her mother saying she was born with black hair, so Charlotte didn't take after her in that respect. In any event, Nina was certain

Jack hadn't examined Charlotte for likenesses. She was just the kid to him.

"Well, whether she looks like him or not, babies have a way of winding themselves around fathers' hearts," Rhonda declared, unable to imagine any other outcome. "He wouldn't want to marry you if he didn't want her."

The marriage offer had certainly come as a surprise. Probably a conditioned response to the situation, Nina had reasoned, guilt leading to a burst of doing the right thing by her. Given time, Jack would undoubtedly rue the impulsive idea.

"It won't last," Nina said, casting a quelling look at Jack's well-meaning supporters and determinedly dampening the little hope that kept squiggling through her.

Rhonda couldn't resist a last word. "Look at it this way. If he's got plenty of money, you could always hire a nanny to take the hassle out of looking after the baby."

A nanny for a kid. Rhonda had hit the nail on the head with that one, Nina thought. It probably would be Jack's solution to avoiding having anything to do with Charlotte. Well, he could think again if he was planning to separate her from her baby so he could have their twosome back without the hassle of being involved in parenting.

Charlotte hiccupped. Nina hoisted her up and gently rubbed her back to bring up wind. No nanny could feed her baby as she could. Jack had better appreciate her position on mothering—and fathering—if he really wanted to consider marriage. It was a family package deal or nothing, as far as Nina was concerned.

If Jack came today—she glanced at the roses. *When* he came today, she needed to get a few things straightened out. He'd better come today if he wanted to show good faith. Sally was taking her home tonight. Nina had no intention of waiting around with Charlotte, hanging onto a hope that might not materialise.

Charlotte burped, then started snuffling around Nina's shoulder for more milk. Nina lowered her onto her other breast and settled back contentedly to let her baby have her fill.

If Jack Gulliver thought he could walk into their lives and take over as he pleased, he was in for a big surprise.

Two hours later he breezed into the ward, radiating goodwill and bearing more gifts. Nina felt her pulse quicken. He had always excited her. She found herself cravenly wishing she'd put on make-up and a sexier nightie than the practical cotton one with the convenient buttons for breastfeeding. Which was absurd in the circumstances.

"I beat the lunch trolley," he said, grinning triumphantly as he set his parcels down on her mobile tray and started removing their contents. "I brought you a chocolate thick shake from McDonald's, that terrine you love—the one with bacon and chicken and pistachio nuts in it—from David Jones's food hall, your favourite Caesar salad, and fresh strawberries and cream to finish up. Enjoy," he commanded, positioning the newly laden tray across the bed for easy accessibility.

She stared at him in amazement, not only that he'd remembered what she liked but had actually gone to the trouble of getting it for her. "The hospital does feed me, you know," she said, struggling against the seduction of being pampered.

"You need appetite tempters, not mass-produced stuff," he argued earnestly. "And none of this will upset the baby. I checked. So you can eat with a clear conscience."

He looked so confident, brimming with bon-homie, his green eyes aglow with a gusto for life. It wasn't fair that he still had the power to dazzle her with his vitality, to ignite a flood of desire with his sizzling sex appeal. It was imperative she keep her head clear and her heart guarded. His words finally filtered through the attraction zone she had to disregard.

"You checked what would upset the baby?" she asked incredulously.

"No excuses for not eating, Nina. You look thin and run-down, and that's not a good state to be in. You need a full store of energy to cope with a new baby."

He was sounding off like an authority, and being altogether too virtuous for someone who wanted nothing to do with babies. "Since when did you become an expert on these matters?'' she asked suspiciously.

"Made a few phone calls last night for some first-hand advice." He grinned again. "I've got plenty of friends ready, willing and able to hand it out."

Determinedly cheerful in the face of disaster, Nina thought, though she had to concede he had made it through about sixteen hours without backing off and he was putting in considerable effort at this point. It won't last, she repeated to herself, but Sally's sales pitch swirled through her mind, whispering she might as well make the most of it while it did. The terrine was definitely a slice of gourmet heaven.

"Thank you, Jack," she said sincerely. "This is very kind and thoughtful of you."

"You're welcome. Go ahead and eat," he urged.

The hospital lunch trolley was wheeled in, and Jack waved it on to Kim and Rhonda. They were served with trays of what they had ordered, and Nina hoped they would be somewhat distracted from being interested spectators to the latest development between her and Jack.

She broke open the packet of crackers that accompanied the terrine and helped herself to a generous slice of the tasty delicacy, highly conscious of Jack watching her, exuding intense satisfaction. It was probably a big mistake accepting anything from him, encouraging him to stick around, Nina thought. It would end badly. But right at this moment, however wrong it was, it felt good having Jack here with her.

He stepped to the bassinette and looked at Charlotte, who was sleeping peacefully. This happy state did not test Jack's paternal staying power. It positively increased his cheerfulness.

"Hi, kid. This is your dad speaking," he said, blithely confident of no reply. "I'm looking after your mum now, so there's nothing for you to worry about. You can dream blissful dreams of plenty."

The terrine was delicious. Nina had to acknowledge Jack had the capacity to be a good provider. And he couldn't blame Charlotte for messing up his chosen career, because that was solidly established. Apart from his earning power, he'd never been in financial difficulties, anyway. His parents had both been in the law profession, wealthy people who'd left a considerable estate to their only child when they died, both of them from heart attacks in their early sixties.

"Worked themselves to death," Jack had remarked offhandedly, and Nina had received the strong impression there had been no great love lost between him and his parents.

Yet he must have been a wanted child. His mother had chosen to have him in her late thirties. Nina figured his parents had probably been disappointed and alienated from Jack when he'd chosen to do manual work rather than follow them into their highbrow profession.

In any event, Jack had no money problems.

He had an attitude problem.

And Nina didn't believe in overnight transformations, however much she might want to. She had seen Jack look benevolently upon babies before, even speak to them benevolently. She knew it to be an act, a social pretence. They were anathema to him.

"Good sleeper, isn't she?" Jack commented, warm approval in his voice.

"She'll probably turn into the baby from hell once I take her home," Nina predicted.

"Well, we'll meet that problem when it comes," he said, clinging to blind optimism.

"Why, Jack?" she demanded. "Why are you even thinking of taking this on? I didn't imagine what you said to me about babies."

His eyes were pained. "Nina, if I could take that back... if I could take back these past eight months, I would. There's been one hell of a hole in my life since you took yourself out of it."

Her heart flipped over. She tore her gaze from his and attacked the lettuce in the Caesar salad. However much he wanted it to be, this was no longer a one-on-one situation. She couldn't answer his needs. She concentrated fiercely on what she was eating. The dressing on the salad was superb. She loved the tangy taste of anchovies.

Jack pulled up the visitor's chair and sat down. "I meant what I wrote on the card with the roses, Nina," he said quietly.

"Sorry." She choked the word out. "I should have thanked you for the flowers. They're very nice."

She kept shovelling the salad down her throat so it wouldn't tighten up. Her stomach wasn't receiving it so well, but she hoped it would soon settle down if she piled enough food into it. She was not—*not* going to let Jack Gulliver twist up her straight thinking or her carefully organised plans or her stomach.

"I've missed you. More than I can say," he went on, undeterred by her lack of enthusiasm. "You were the best thing that ever happened to me, Nina. I don't want to lose you again."

He was remembering how it was. That was forever gone. No point in thinking it could be recaptured, not with Charlotte in the picture. Nina relentlessly crunched some croutons. They were more substantial than lettuce.

"You disappeared so quickly," he complained. "One week. Just one week, and you were gone. No forwarding address from where you'd been living. You didn't even work out your notice on the job you left. No one had a clue to your new whereabouts."

Pure luck, she thought, seeing Sally's advertisement for a seamstress in the *Herald* the day after the critical argument with Jack. She wondered briefly if it had been good luck or bad luck.

"You made your stand, Jack," she reminded him, her eyes sharply scanning his. "You said last night I didn't give you a choice. I didn't think you gave me one. Can you honestly say, if I'd confronted you with my pregnancy one week after that argument, you would have reacted as you seem to be reacting now?''

He hesitated, searching his mind for an honest response. ''I love you, Nina. I would have done whatever you wanted of me.''

A weight lifted off her heart. At least he wouldn't have suggested an abortion. The hope squiggled again. Love sounded good. Love sounded wonderful. On the other hand, his response was entirely concentrated on her, which left out the baby.

Nina shook her head sadly. ''It doesn't work like that, Jack. It's too one-sided. We had a lot of joy together....''

''Yes, we did,'' he said eagerly, his eyes simmering with memories.

Sex, Nina thought. Wild, uninhibited, stupendous, passionate sex. Total absorption in each other. That was what he was remembering and that was what he wanted back. She took a deep breath and deliberately dashed the highly distracting ardour emanating from him.

''I don't want to live with every bit of joy being whittled away by your resentment of the baby, Jack.''

He raised a hand in solemn fervour. ''Nina, I swear to you I can accommodate the kid.''

Nina gritted her teeth. *Accommodate the kid!* How dared he talk about Charlotte like that? It was hopeless. Absolutely hopeless. She picked up a strawberry and bit the fruit off its stalk, seething through its juice. Jack Gulliver might be the sexiest man alive, but he wasn't worth a father's bootlace. She shot him down with her eyes.

"If you're thinking of hiring a nanny—"

"A nanny! Who said anything about hiring a nanny?" He looked upset, frowning belligerently. "No kid of mine is going to be brought up by nannies. If that's your plan, Nina, I've got to say right now I disapprove of it."

Nina was so stunned, she popped another strawberry into her mouth, and the question, "You do?" became something of a gobble.

"I most certainly do. My parents left me with nannies until I was seven years old and then they turfed me off to boarding school."

"That's terrible!"

"We are not going to do that, Nina."

"Oh, no!" She grabbed another strawberry, fascinated by these revelations about Jack's childhood.

He stood up and pointed at the bassinette. "This kid is going to be brought up right."

She nodded agreement, her mouth full of juicy fruit, her eyes feasting on a vision of Jack as a dedicated and devoted parent.

He leaned over and kissed her forehead. "Must get to work now. I've got a shipment of stuff coming in. Keep eating, Nina. You need building up. Put some cream on the strawberries. It's good for the kid."

She nodded again, totally dumbfounded by this turn of events.

He paused by the bassinette. "See you tonight, Charlie girl. Be good for your mum. We've got to get her straightened out on a few things."

He was almost out the door before Nina remembered. "Sally is picking me up tonight," she called after him. "I'm going home, Jack."

He halted, looking at her with determined authority. "Correction. I'm picking you up. I've already fixed it with Sally. Very understanding woman, Sally. She let me into your granny flat so I could provision your fridge properly. No more skimping on meals, Nina."

He left, having taken over as he pleased. Nina felt steamrollered. Maybe she did need straightening out. Hope jiggled in her heart and danced around her mind as she poured some cream onto the strawberries. She looked at Charlotte, who was still sleeping peacefully.

"Well, kid," she said giddily. "Maybe you've got a dad after all." Then she sobered up and added, "But I'll believe it when I see it."

CHAPTER SIX

IT WAS strange, sitting beside Jack in his car, driving across the city. Nina felt she was in a time warp, as though the past eight months hadn't happened. Same big, four-wheel-drive Range Rover he had owned then, same sense of being king of the road with all the lower traffic around them, same man in control of where they went, drawing an intense physical awareness of him, same feeling of intimacy, enclosed in a world of their own.

To shake off the eerie feeling, Nina kept glancing around to check that Charlotte was, indeed, with them, securely tucked into her capsule and undisturbed by her new and strange surroundings. Life had moved on, and Charlotte added another dimension to it.

Jack had expertly anchored the capsule on the rear seat. He'd had his vehicle fitted for it today, learning where to put the bolt from the safety harness and get everything adjusted properly. Nina was amazed at his forethought. At least in this practical sense he had accepted Charlotte.

"Stop worrying, Nina. There's no problem." He gave her a reassuring smile as he caught her glancing at the rear seat again. "Babies always sleep in moving vehicles."

"How do you know that?"

His smile turned lopsided. "A guy I know drove around most of one night with his kid. His wife was desperate for sleep, and it was a surefire way to stop the baby from crying."

"Maybe there was something wrong with the baby."

"Just colic."

He spoke so matter-of-factly, yet Nina was acutely conscious of the problems he listed and how they could affect their relationship. So far, Jack had only ever seen Charlotte asleep, like a serene little doll, demanding only a token acknowledgment. It was easy to think nothing much had changed. She was guilty of it herself, sitting beside him, remembering how it had been together...before Charlotte.

But they weren't going out on a date and they weren't going home to make love. Tension knotted her stomach as she wondered about Jack's expectations of tonight. Did he think they could pick up from where they had left off eight months ago?

He hadn't tried to kiss her, as yet. Not properly. Nor had he really touched her except in courteous and caring support. She stared at his hands, lightly guiding the steering wheel. Perhaps it was from his love of working with wood, bringing out the beauty of its grain. Jack had wonderfully sensitive hands. As much as Nina craved the physical reassurance of his love, it was too soon to let him resume their former intimacy.

Too soon in several senses. Her body needed recovery time from the ordeal of giving birth. Apart from which, Nina felt the need to test Jack's commitment to Charlotte before involving herself too closely with him. She couldn't **risk** accepting it on faith alone. The road to hell was paved with good intentions.

They were driving into the harbour tunnel now. Once they emerged on the north side, it wasn't far to Lane Cove, where Sally's house and business were handily situated to draw clients from both the northern and western suburbs of Sydney. Nina hoped Jack wasn't anticipating staying overnight in her granny flat. She hoped he wasn't assuming everything was settled between them. It wasn't. Maybe she should make that clear right now.

Something rolled against her feet as the Rover headed down the tunnel. She leaned over to pick it up. A can of dog meat. Nina stared at it, inwardly recoiling from what it meant. Jack still had the dog.

"Sorry about that," he said, glancing over with a rueful grimace. "Must have escaped from one of the shopping bags. Better put it in the glove box, out of the way."

She did as he suggested, wishing Jack wasn't so attached to the mongrel dog he'd rescued from the RSPCA. It was big and fierce, and she was frightened of it. Jack had trained it to be a great watchdog, which was important, since the furniture he worked on was very valuable. Although he insisted Spike's bark was worse than his bite, Nina had never been able to bring herself to pat it and play with it as Jack did.

Maybe it was because she hadn't had any familiarity with dogs during her upbringing. Which reminded her... "How come you never told me about your childhood, Jack?"

He shrugged. "No joy in recalling misery, Nina."

It was a fair answer. She hadn't detailed her childhood to him, either, only telling him her parents had divorced and she'd lived with her grandmother until she'd come to Sydney to go to design school. Since her family—if you could call it that—lived hundreds of kilometres away at Port Macquarie, the question of visiting them had been easily put aside.

Besides, with his own parents dead, Jack was not family minded. He'd never pressed her on the subject, accepting her independence as naturally as he took his own for granted. There had been no reason to tell him she had been an unwanted burden to everyone. It didn't do much for her self-esteem. Jack had accepted her as the person she was—no concern about her background—and that was how she liked it.

"Did you have a dog when you were a boy?" she asked, switching to her earlier thought.

"No. My parents wouldn't allow it. Too much trouble." He flashed her a wry smile. "*I* was too much trouble, let alone a dog."

So he'd been a burden, too, though not an unwanted one.

"Where I went to school, the caretaker had a dog. He let me play with it," Jack added in fond reminiscence. "Honey. That was her name. A Labrador. One year she had nine pups. I would have given anything for one of those pups."

Nina smothered a sigh. Jack was not about to be separated from Spike. Another problem. How could she let that ferocious dog anywhere near Charlotte? There were too many horror stories about dogs mauling children for Nina to even contemplate taking a chance with it.

They were out of the tunnel and heading up the Warringah Freeway. Jack would normally take the Willoughby Road turn-off to go to his home at Roseville Chase. He had a lovely place, Nina reflected, overlooking Echo Point and Middle Harbour. He'd turned the triple garage into his main work area, but he did the finishing in the rumpus room. It was an ideal set-up for Jack, but a child would certainly put a spoke in it.

They passed the turn-off and zoomed along to the Gore Hill Freeway. Nina steeled herself to spell out the situation as she saw it. Jack had to understand that giving an off-the-cuff commitment was not enough for her. She needed some very solid follow-up before she could even think of getting herself deeply entangled with him. She was about to open her mouth when he spoke first.

"Every kid should have a dog," he declared, nodding over the idea. He looked to her for approval. "Maybe a little one to begin with. I've heard that miniature fox terriers make great pets."

Miniature sounded good. "I think there's a few other things to settle first," she warned, and they weren't in the miniature category, either. Jack was leaping ahead with apparently blind disregard of the adjustments he'd have to make to his lifestyle.

"Sure," he agreed blithely. "I won't rush you, Nina. Sally reckoned it would take at least six weeks to organise a dream wedding. I wouldn't do you out of a dream."

Her mind freaked out. "Jack!" She looked at him in horror. "I don't believe in shotgun marriages."

He frowned at her. "No-one's pointing a gun at my head, Nina."

"You wouldn't have thought of marriage except for the baby," she said accusingly.

"That's not true. I was going to ask you to live with me the very night we had that damned argument. Same thing."

"It's not the same thing at all!"

"It is for me." His green eyes flashed intense conviction. "You're the only woman I've ever wanted to live with, Nina."

"You're forgetting something, aren't you?" she asked angrily. "I come with a child."

"It's because I'm taking our kid into consideration that I think marriage is a better idea," he answered with controlled patience. "Kids like to feel secure with their mum and dad."

"That's all very well in theory," Nina retorted fiercely. "It doesn't work out so neatly in practice. More than one in every three marriages ends in divorce. Where are the kids then?"

He sighed and slanted her a sympathetic look. "I know you're speaking from your own personal experience, Nina. It must have hurt a lot when your parents divorced..."

No, it didn't. The hurt came long before the divorce.

"But that's no reason not to give us a chance," he went on. "We're different people."

"I wouldn't be with you now if I wasn't prepared to give it a chance, Jack," she said tightly. "But will you please stop assuming I'm ready to commit myself and Charlotte to you? I'm not."

Silence.

Nina could feel Jack brooding, searching for ways and means around her doubts and fears. It set her nerves on edge. She didn't want pressure. She couldn't cope with it right now. While life didn't hang out guarantees for anything, trust did require time to build.

It came as a shock when Jack pulled the Range Rover over to the kerb outside Sally's house and cut the engine. Nina had lost track of where they were. Home! Her heart fluttered in agitation. She hoped Jack wasn't going to be difficult, wanting more than she could give.

He released his seat belt and turned to her, reaching out to gently cup her cheek and capture her attention. "Nina..." His eyes glowed with commanding intensity, and his voice was furred with deep emotion. "I love you. I don't say that lightly. Let me show you...."

He leaned over. Before she could even think of stopping him, his mouth claimed hers with a seductive, tender yearning that melted any resistance she might have mustered if it had been a storming kiss. It was so gentle, so sweet, a sensitive tasting, begging a response, not trying to force one.

She ached for more, the emptiness of all the lonely months without him surging into a desperate need to be filled, to have doubts and fears obliterated by a flood of love so overwhelming it could carry everything in its stride. Her lips moved instinctively, encouraging, inviting, hungry for what he was offering, blindly seeking the reassurance of the passion she had known with him.

She lifted her hand to his chest, loving the warmth and strength she could feel through the light fabric of his shirt, the exciting thud of his heart, beating hard and fast with his need for her. It *was* the same as before.

Intoxicated by the wonderful familiarity of touching him again, Nina slid her hand over the smooth roundness of his shoulder, up the strong column of his neck and tunnelled her fingers through the thick springiness of his hair, exulting in the tactile reality of what had become only a haunting dream.

Jack... his mouth filling hers with enthralling sensation, feasting on her eager response, drawing on the desire that had always exploded between them. It flowed now, a torrent of wanting that craved fulfilment. Her body trembled with the force of it, weakness draining through her legs, ripples of arousal spreading to her stomach, her breasts straining to be caressed and held.

Slowly, reluctantly, Jack leashed the power of the passion they shared, leaving her still pulsing with sensation as he drew back, breathing roughly yet stroking her cheek and lips with feather-light fingertips. She dizzily opened her eyes, breathless, wavering between a protest at his parting from her and a plea for what had started to be finished.

He looked anguished. "I could have been with you all this time...."

She didn't want to look back. She wanted...

"I would have been, Nina, if only you'd told me."

Was that true? Had she robbed them of what should have been? This magic that was theirs?

His eyes swore it was so. "I wouldn't have let anything get in the way of what we have together."

Her desire-drenched mind thrilled to the constancy he avowed...until slowly, inexorably, it grasped the logic of what he was saying.

He wouldn't let Charlotte get in the way.

Which surely meant he would resent their child if she did. It was all too easy to forget her, not take her into account at all while she slept, a silent, non-interfering presence. But it wouldn't stay like that.

"Charlotte." It was a husky croak, loaded with the guilt of her own forgetfulness.

"She's okay for a minute or two."

"No." Nina scrabbled for the release mechanism on her seat belt, jerking her head away from Jack's tempting touch and dropping her gaze from the heart-searing heat of his. "I don't want to talk about this now, Jack. I want to get unpacked and settled into my flat again."

"I wasn't blaming you for the decision you made, Nina, just regretting the waste of time," he said softly. "It's made me very conscious of not wasting any more of it."

"Fine! Let's get moving."

The seat belt zipped away. She opened the passenger door and leapt out of the cabin before Jack could detain her further. Her legs almost crumpled under her. She had to hang onto the door to steady herself. The physical upheaval of giving birth to a baby was debilitating enough without adding sexual and emotional upheavals.

Nina instantly vowed to keep Jack at a firm distance until she could gauge his real reactions to having a baby in their lives. She didn't want to be torn in two by conflicting loves. If she gave in to what she felt for Jack now, it would only make everything ten times worse if she had to part from him for Charlotte's sake.

"Are you all right?" he asked in concern.

"Yes." *Apart from being hopelessly vulnerable to you,* she added, silently railing at her weakness. She scooped her handbag from the floor in front of the passenger seat, shut the door and leaned against it, willing herself to be strong as Jack alighted from the driver's side.

He didn't press her. Much to Nina's relief, he set about the business of releasing Charlotte's capsule and collecting her suitcase from the back of the Rover. He carried both, leaving Nina to lead the way down the side path to her flat at the back of Sally's house. Her legs were still shaky, but she managed the walk with some dignity, grateful that Jack had assumed the role of porter.

All the lights were on, a welcoming gesture from Sally, no doubt. Nina unlocked the door and waved him inside, acutely conscious of the danger inherent in letting Jack invade her home, yet aware of how unfair and ungracious it would be to deny him entry. He would respect her wishes, she assured herself. All she had to do was take control of the situation and remain firm, no matter how persuasive Jack set out to be.

"Straight into the bedroom?" he asked quietly, nodding at Charlotte.

"Yes, please," she whispered, flushing at the reminder of having shared a bedroom with him many times in the past.

Having been let in by Sally to provision the refrigerator earlier today, Jack was clearly familiar with the layout of the flat. Nina watched him manoeuvre the capsule and suitcase down the narrow hall, past the bathroom and laundry. The bedroom door was open. There was no need for Nina to accompany him or follow him. Better to keep her distance.

She stepped into the kitchenette, feeling more protected by the cupboards and countertops that hemmed the limited moving space. Having checked the electric kettle and found it full of water, she switched it on. After all the trouble Jack had gone to for her today, it was impossible to send him away without offering him at least a cup of tea.

As she waited for the water to boil, Nina took a deep breath in an attempt to calm her skittering nerves and flicked her gaze around the living area she had made her own, needing to regain the sense of independence it had given her. Jack probably thought it was small and cramped, but she had it arranged to suit her convenience.

The two-seater cane lounge and matching armchairs were grouped on the window side of the living room, a coffee table handily placed. On the other side was her sewing machine. Behind it on the wall was a huge corkboard, organised to hold all her reels of cotton, scissors, measuring sticks and other tools of her trade. At the end of the room was the television set and her sound system, so she could watch a program or listen to music as she worked or relaxed.

The mottled beige tiles on the floor were easy to keep clean. She had made the cushion covers and curtains herself in a bright, fresh fabric patterned in lemon and white and lime green. A bowl of brilliant lemon chrysanthemums sat on the coffee table, a welcome home gift from Sally, Nina figured. She'd left Jack's roses at the hospital for Rhonda and Kim to enjoy. An arrangement of three dozen was difficult to transport.

Jack had probably frowned over the wooden planks under the legs of the dining table. They effectively raised it to a convenient height for measuring and cutting fabric. She didn't use the table for meals, preferring to keep it for work. Normally she perched on a stool at the kitchen counter to eat or drink. But that didn't mean she wasn't looking after herself properly.

She heard Jack coming from the bedroom and hastily set out cups and saucers. By opening the refrigerator door, she effectively blocked the path into the kitchenette. Nina only meant to get out milk and direct Jack to the other side of the kitchen counter. However, the stacked contents of the refrigerator completely distracted her.

"All quiet on the Western Front," Jack declared cheerfully.

Nina barely heard him. Apart from an incredible array of delicatessen goods loading up the shelves, the meat tray contained great slabs of steak, at least a dozen rashers of bacon, piles of chops and sausages, and the vegetable containers were chock-a-block with items from the greengrocers.

"I'll never eat all this," she said dazedly.

"I'll help you," came the confident reply.

Warning tingles ran down her spine. Nina forgot about the milk. She shut the refrigerator door and swung around to face a more pressing problem. Jack shot his most dazzling smile at her across the counter that separated them, and Nina felt her resolution fraying at the edges. He was making it so hard for her to hang onto common sense. Desperation drove a steely tone into her voice.

"Are you planning on having meals with me, Jack?"

His eyebrows lifted in appeal. "I thought I'd come over after work and cook dinner for us. It'll give you a rest in between the two evening feeds for the kid."

"That's very considerate of you." He was taking over. Just walking in and taking over as he pleased. Intent on claiming whatever time she had free from the baby. Nina gritted her teeth in determined resistance to his infiltration tactics. "Are you thinking of cooking breakfast for me, too?"

"Well, uh..." He hesitated, taking in the dangerous glitter in her eyes. "It's not a good idea?" he asked cautiously.

"Not if you're assuming you can stay overnight with me any time you like," she answered angrily.

"Not any time, Nina. Naturally I'll do whatever's best for you," he hastily assured her, then changed his expression to anxious concern. "But I am worried about tonight. Everyone says the first night home with a new baby is scary. No expert to call on..."

"And you consider yourself an expert?" Nina heard her voice rise to a shrill note.

"I meant it's lonely," he swiftly amended. "I don't like to think of you being by yourself, Nina. What if you have a bad night with the kid? No one to talk to..."

"No one to hold me and comfort me and kiss everything better. Is that the idea, Jack?" Wanting to satisfy his hunger for her, never mind what had to be done for the baby.

He frowned at her brittle manner. "I just want to be here for you, Nina."

He sounded so genuine. The look of caring in his eyes was almost her undoing. Her heart seemed to be pounding in her ears. She wanted his love, wanted to feel it surround her, seep into her, possess her to the point of losing herself entirely in him. But he only wanted to be here for her, and that wasn't enough. It simply wasn't enough.

If only he cared as much about Charlotte.

She closed her eyes, gathered the will to sort through her priorities again, knew she couldn't battle with her dilemma any more tonight and took the only escape route open to her.

"I want you to go now, Jack."

"But, Nina . . ."

She opened her eyes, anguished by his persistence. "Please."

He looked hurt and bewildered. "Why? What have I done wrong?"

"Don't argue with me," she cried in desperation. Frantic to end the torment he stirred, she rushed to the door and opened it for him to leave. "Please. It's been a long day for me. I need time and space for myself, Jack."

He moved reluctantly, his eyes urgently scanning hers, wanting a reason for what he saw as incomprehensible behaviour. He lifted his hands, gesturing his willingness to appease whatever was troubling her. "What if—?"

"No!" She shook her head vehemently. "It's too much, too soon. Good night, Jack. Thank you for bringing us home, but I really do need you to go now."

"All right," he said gently, seeing she was too stressed to discuss the matter further. "Good night, Nina. Say good night to the kid for me."

The kid.

He left.

Nina closed the door after him and promptly burst into tears.

CHAPTER SEVEN

WHAT had he done wrong?

The question plagued Jack as he roamed disconsolately around the collection of antiques that had been delivered this afternoon. Normally he would be excited by the challenge of restoring the damaged pieces, keenly studying how it could best be done. He couldn't find any enthusiasm for it tonight. Nothing was working for him. Except for his dog, who was trailing him around, offering his loyal companionship.

"She shut me out again, Spike," he said, heaving a woebegone sigh.

Man's best friend cocked his head, giving him a doleful look of sympathy, then sprang up to rest his front paws on Jack's chest, his tongue out, ready to lick everything better if Jack obliged by bending his head close enough. The weight of the huge, black and white shaggy beast would have knocked most people down, but Spike knew how to balance nicely when it was a matter of love and respect.

Jack looked fondly on him. "You're a great dog, Spike, but I've got to tell you, your breath isn't as sweet as Nina's."

A whistling whine, begging favour.

Jack gave him a rueful smile and ruffled the
fur behind his ears, earning a look of adoration
that let Jack know Spike was absolutely steadfast
in his love and devotion, no confusing or ob-
scure responses and reactions coming from him.
Jack was the central focus of his world, and there
was no shifting him from that outlook. Spike
knew what was good for him.

It was a pity people weren't more like dogs,
Jack thought, brooding over all he'd done today
to get things right between him and Nina. He was
good for her. He knew he was. Why didn't she
recognise it? Why wasn't she welcoming it? What
more could he have done to show her he meant
what he said?

"Maybe dogs are smarter than people," he
confided to Spike. "People should think less and
trust their instincts more."

Spike panted agreement.

Jack reflected, with perfect justification, that
there had been no confusion at all in Nina's response when he'd kissed her. He'd felt the electric
current of desire charging through both of them,
highly mutual, fantastically mutual. No possible
mistake about it. Nina still wanted him. Whatever
was muddling her mind was a frustrating mystery,
but her body was definitely in harmony with his.

Jack felt himself stir just thinking about it.
He'd been celibate for so long, all his hormones
were zinging with excitement at the promise of
knowing satisfaction again. Real satisfaction.
Special satisfaction. It had always been special

with Nina. She was his woman, pure and simple. Somehow he had to work out how to convince her he was her man. There was no point in even looking at any of this furniture until he'd figured out what to do about his problem with Nina.

With more than one appetite reawakened, Jack realised the empty feeling inside him could be attributed to a more pedantic hunger. "Let's go and find something to eat, Spike."

With a bright yelp of encouragement, the part kelpie, part collie, part Doberman, part several other breeds including, Jack suspected, great Dane, leapt down and bounded over to the door that led into the house. Why couldn't people be as simple and direct? Jack wondered with another niggle of frustration. He and Spike had no problem understanding each other.

They headed for the kitchen together. It was handily situated to what had once been the triple garage. Jack didn't mind his two apprentices ducking in to make coffee or get a snack. He'd always figured work flowed more easily if people felt at home. Sharing meals had seemed a good way of getting Nina to feel at home with him.

Too much, too soon, she had said, but he couldn't see why. The path to getting back together again was going to be very difficult if she kept shutting him out.

Jack opened the refrigerator and took out one of the meaty bones he'd got from the butcher that morning. "Here you are, Spike. It's your favourite. Ham."

Spike clutched it eagerly in his jaws, growling approval and appreciation, wagging his bushy tail in delight as he retired to his corner of the kitchen. He settled down, his position protected from attack from behind and on the flank by the two walls, his fiercely watchful eyes defying any approach from the front. Spike jealously guarded his bones, instinctively suspicious of any movement towards him. Protection was top priority. Even Jack was persona non grata if he moved too close.

Too close. The thought caught and held. Was that what Nina was guarding against, letting him get too close? Protecting herself and the baby in case he hadn't really changed his attitude about children? She kept harping back to that argument. Understandable enough, since she'd been feeding it through her brain for the past eight months.

Jack pondered this possibility as he collected some cheese and pickles, took some crackers from the pantry and settled down at the bar counter to chew over the situation. It could be the kid confusing Nina, distorting what was perfectly plain and straightforward to him.

Basically the kid was a side product of what they felt for each other. Naturally he accepted it, now that he knew about it. What kind of man would he be if he didn't? He would have accepted it eight months ago, too. Nina had got herself all cock-eyed about that.

Maybe she didn't want to share it with him. Like Spike with his bone. He reconsidered Nina's behaviour in the same light as his dog's current attitude—wary and watchful and ready to pounce on anything questionable and fight like the devil. Possessive and protective. It could explain a lot.

Though there was one difference. Jack knew he could still get to Nina on a one-to-one level. Maybe that was what she was afraid of, knowing he could slip past her defences despite being hell-bent on protecting the kid. Yet what was she expecting him to do? Take the kid away from her? Be jealous of her natural mother love? It was ridiculous.

"You can vouch for my character, can't you, Spike?"

The dog looked up, alert and attentive.

"Have I ever done you wrong?"

Spike growled at the idea.

"Of course not. You'd defend me to the death, wouldn't you?"

A bark of assent.

"We know I'm the salt of the earth. And Nina should know, too. But if she's gnawing at that old bone of contention all the time... It could be the answer, Spike."

A darker growl.

"You're right. She should know better. Thanks for helping me out, Spike. You're a great source of inspiration."

Understanding that the conversation was over and having given satisfaction, man's best friend returned to feeding his own satisfaction. He knew there was more in a bone than there was on the surface.

The idea of Nina shutting him out because she didn't trust him to behave as a father should did not sit well with Jack. It was extremely offensive to him. If that was Nina's belief, he had to set her straight. He could be as good a father as anyone else. Better. After all, he'd heard most of the complaints new parents made about each other, so he could work out how to circumvent them.

First thing tomorrow he'd call Maurice and arrange to have nappy-changing lessons from Ingrid. The criticism that fathers were inept or useless at such a task was not going to apply to him. As for Nina scoffing about him being an expert on babies, well, why couldn't he become one? There had to be plenty of books on baby problems.

He'd much prefer Nina to be leaning on him for advice and support than shutting him out. In fact, the more she leaned on him, the more likely she was to want what he wanted. Once they could make love again, Jack was sure everything would be fine between them. The fabulous fusion of their bodies into one, the glorious sense of ecstatic fulfilment, the deep intimacy of sharing the excitement and the aftermath . . . Jack wanted all that very badly.

This kid thing was not going to beat him.

Or break them up.

Feeling much more cheerful about the situation, Jack cut off a big chunk of cheese, spread it with pickles and bit into it with relish. Tomorrow was another day. Tomorrow he would knock Nina's worries about his fatherly fitness right on the head. She wouldn't shut him out again. No, sir.

"Here comes your dad, kid," he said out loud, enjoying the ring of it. "Here comes your dad."

CHAPTER EIGHT

THE knock on the connecting door from the flat to the house had to be Sally's. Nina smiled as she called, "Come in!" It was eight-thirty, the time Sally usually checked in with her each morning to discuss the business of the day. The return to routine gave Nina a comforting sense of normality and security. She needed it after the tumult of uncertainty Jack had stirred last night.

The door near the far corner of the living room opened, and Sally popped her head around, waggling her highly mobile eyebrows. "I'm not disturbing anything?"

Nina shook her head. "I'm all organised. Just washing up breakfast things. Have you got time for a cup of coffee?"

"If it's no trouble." Having been welcomed, Sally sailed in, looking sunnily superb in a wheat-gold suit. She perched on the stool by the kitchen counter, her bright hazel eyes alight with curiosity and interest. "How's the babe this morning?"

"No problems so far. She only woke to be fed once during the night. I couldn't ask for a more contented baby."

"Let's hope it lasts."

For more reasons than one, Nina thought as she put the kettle on and spooned instant coffee into a mug for Sally. Jack might come to love a good baby, though babyhood was only the start of a long, trying journey with children. Would Jack last the distance?

She pushed the worry aside and gave Sally a warm smile. "Thanks for organising the nappy service for me."

"Piece of cake."

Nina waved at the coffee table. "And the lovely flowers. They're perfect."

"Oh, Jack bought those. I only put them in the bowl." She gave Nina an arch look. "That guy is worth marrying, Nina. He cares a lot about you."

"Mmm, we'll see," Nina answered off-handedly. The kettle whistled. Glad of the distraction, Nina turned away to make the coffee to Sally's taste. "Any bookings for me?" she asked, turning the conversation to business. She didn't want to discuss Jack. Her feelings about him swung from wild longing to helpless despair.

Sally was not slow on reading signals. She obligingly picked up the cue. "I've tried to keep this week clear for you, but weddings always throw up last-minute little traumas. Juliette Hardwick has lost weight and wants her dress taken in. I've scheduled a fitting for seven o'clock tonight. Can do?"

"Of course."

If Jack came for dinner, as he planned, he'd
have to understand she wasn't always available
when he wanted her to be. Most clients came after
normal working hours. It was the only time they
were free, and Nina had to accommodate them.
Running one's own business was a lot different
from working for someone else. Customers came
first. The baby's needs came ahead of Jack's,
too. Nina could see his patience running out very
quickly.

"Tomorrow's free," Sally continued, "but
Friday night Belinda Pinkerton and her mother
and her three bridesmaids are coming for a con-
sultation. Seven-thirty. They want your advice
on what would best suit them." Sally rolled her
eyes expressively. "Could be a big job in it for
you, Nina."

It was a thrilling thought. Nina grinned, her
eyes dancing with excitement. "I'll sharpen up
my sales pitch."

"Nothing like a complete showcase to ad-
vertise your talent," Sally encouraged. "Belinda
likes dramatic. Think about it. And the
Pinkertons have serious money to spend, so think
big."

"Great!"

Sally drank some of her coffee then casually
remarked, "I would have dropped in last night
but I didn't want to intrude on anything private."

Nina's burst of pleasure dimmed. She just
didn't know where she was going with Jack.

Sally noted the change and grimaced. "I hope I didn't do the wrong thing in letting Jack bring you home."

"No."

"He was very eager."

"Yes."

The monosyllabic replies drew a deep sigh from Sally. "I know it's none of my business, Nina, but the guy seemed very sincere. I had a long talk with him after we left the hospital the other night. He's dead-set on marrying you."

"Maybe."

Sally gave her a sharp, penetrating look. "You don't want him?"

Nina winced. "It's not that."

"Well, if you're worried about the business, Jack assured me he'd respect and support any outlet you wanted for your creativity. He said he understood how you felt about it and knew how important it was for your own sense of achievement and fulfilment. The guy really impressed me, Nina. I don't think you'd have any trouble with him on that score."

Sally was right. Jack wouldn't interfere with any opportunities that came her way. He valued his own work and would apply the same value to hers. It was only the time spent on the baby he'd resent.

"When he was here yesterday, he noted how you'd raised the table and said he'd make you one that fitted all your work requirements," Sally went on. "Save you from getting back problems."

Nina couldn't help smiling. Jack would enjoy getting it right for her. He was quite obsessive about getting things right. Unfortunately, babies and children threw unpredictable spanners into perfect plans. Could Jack learn to live with that? Her smile drooped into a grimace. He'd been totally fed up with the way his friends' baby had disrupted the infamous dinner party.

"I'd snaffle him if I were you," Sally said confidentially. "The guy is pure gold. He's got money. He's got brains. He's got great muscles. And he's not going to mess with our partnership."

Nina sighed and confessed the wretched truth. "He doesn't want children, Sally. That's why I broke up with him in the first place."

Sally's eyebrows disappeared into her flyaway fringe. "He turned his back on you when you got pregnant?" she squawked in outrage.

"No. I didn't tell him I was pregnant. I knew he didn't want children. He'd told me so in no uncertain terms."

Sally ruminated over these facts as she finished her coffee. She set her mug down and gave Nina the benefit of her wisdom. "Well, he hasn't exactly been put off by Charlotte, has he? Why didn't he run the other way once he found out you'd had his baby?"

Nina shrugged helplessly. "He still wants me. I don't think Charlotte is real to him yet. He remembers how it was between us and he wants that back."

"Hmm." Sally clacked her perfectly manicured fingernails on the counter. "Is he coming to visit this evening?"

"That was the plan. If he hasn't had second thoughts."

"Right!" Sally's authority finger shot out to emphasise points. "Leave Charlotte with him while you deal with Juliette Hardwick. If he wants to skip out of minding the baby, he's history. If he takes it on, he'll start finding out Charlotte is real. Put him to the test, Nina."

Having settled the matter to her satisfaction, Sally slid off the stool, supremely confident of pertinent results.

"But it mightn't prove anything," Nina argued, not liking the idea of leaving Jack in charge of her baby. "Charlotte sleeps most of the time."

"It's a question of attitude," Sally claimed, making a jaunty exit. She paused at the door for a curtain line. "And don't forget to give him a reward if he does good. I'm a great believer in the reward system. It encourages performance."

The door closed.

Right! Nina thought, mentally girding her loins. There was no good to be gained in mushing around with negative pessimism. If she wanted decisive answers, risks had to be taken. If Jack came tonight, she *would* leave Charlotte with him. After all, he was her father. His reaction to the idea of being left in sole charge of a baby should tell her something.

Attitude.

It should be a dead give-away.

CHAPTER NINE

A GLANCE at her watch warned Nina to stop dithering. It was almost five o'clock. Jack finished work at four. She wasn't quite sure what his plan was, but it didn't take long to get from Roseville Chase to Lane Cove. She wanted to be ready for him. For tonight's appointment with Juliette Hardwick, as well.

She always wore black for business. It was classy while also being unobtrusive. It was important for the women being dressed for a wedding to outshine everyone else. Since it was Nina's job to ensure they achieved that result, she didn't want her own appearance to be a distraction. Black was also the perfect foil to show up their dresses in the mirror as she moved around them, tucking and pinning.

With having to breastfeed Charlotte, it was far more practical for her to wear a button-through tunic, but vanity kept pulling her towards the silky two-piece, which featured a cowl neckline and a gold-link belt. It was definitely her sexiest outfit, soft and swishy, the fabric clinging to her curves, accentuating her femininity.

She had worn loose clothes through most of her pregnancy. Now that she had her figure back, more or less, the temptation to really feel like a woman again argued against common sense. Besides, Jack had seen her looking a frump in the hospital. It wouldn't hurt to remind him of how she could look—a sort of welcome, and a reward if he really was as good as his word about being a dad for Charlotte.

She wasn't sure how far a reward should go at this stage. Sally did have a point. Some positive encouragement might help to establish a more positive attitude. It was worth trying, anyway. If Jack saw her making an effort for him, he might make more of an effort with Charlotte.

Decision made, Nina whipped her favoured outfit off its hanger and quickly pulled it on. Her waist wasn't quite back to normal, but her breasts were bigger, so her figure still balanced in a satisfactory fashion. She slipped on a pair of soft gold slippers and hunted through her earrings for the black and gold dangly set that complemented her short hairstyle.

She'd washed and blow-dried her hair into perfect shape earlier this afternoon. The longer sections on either side of her face now curved smoothly along her cheekline. It was a sophisticated style, cleverly shaped to her head and cut higher at the back to accentuate the curve of skull and neck. A gamine-style fringe softened the overall sleek severity of the cut and served to make more of a feature of her large, dark eyes.

In keeping with Sally's policy of always looking good, Nina had taken time with her make-up, using both a light and dark grey shading to add

emphasis to her eyes. Her thick black lashes
looked even more lustrous with mascara. She'd
balanced deep red lipstick with a subtle appli-
cation of toning blusher, making her cheekbones
slightly more dramatic. Sally insisted that hands
were important, too, so a matching red varnish
glossed her well-kept nails.

Now that her hair was short, Nina enjoyed
wearing earrings. She had a long neck, and they
really added style and made a statement with
whatever she was wearing. Having found the pair
she wanted and fastened them to her lobes, Nina
felt a definite lift in spirits as she surveyed her
reflection in the mirror. Not bad. Not bad at all.
She grinned at herself. Jack would see a big difference between yesterday and today.

Not that she wanted to encourage him too
much, more laying a promise on the line if he
was prepared to toe it where Charlotte was concerned. No mother without daughter. A package
deal. And Charlotte was not to be short-changed.
Nina was determined on that.

She moved over to the double bed where the
capsule occupied one side, propped around by
pillows for extra safety. Leaning over the snugly
sleeping baby, she inhaled the fresh, sweet scent
of her. It had been a delight bathing Charlotte
this afternoon, tiny arms splashing, legs kicking,
her eyes wide open, staring up at Nina as though
querying the experience while obviously enjoying it. The world was so new to her. Nina

hoped nothing would spoil it for her daughter for a long, long time.

She moved quietly out of the bedroom and was passing the kitchenette when the knock on the door came, startling her into an abrupt halt. Her heartbeat accelerated with a hop, skip and jump. It had to be Jack. Fate had dictated that their paths cross again. She silently begged not to be disappointed as she composed herself as best she could and took the last few steps to admit the father of her child.

With a hopeful little smile appealing to all that was good in Jack, she opened the door. The same kind of smile was waiting for her, but she barely saw it. Her heart contracted at the sheer male vitality that hit her. Jack was dressed in jeans and a cream and navy body shirt, and his tall, muscular frame seemed to leap at her.

He'd had his hair trimmed, and his face looked so clean-cut and handsome, Nina couldn't help staring, drinking in all his attractive features, the high, wide forehead punctuated by strongly arched eyebrows, eyes of deep river green sweeping over her with drowning intensity, the striking sculpture of his nose and cheekbones and the teasing sensuality of his full-lipped mouth. She could smell the spicy aftershave lotion he had splashed on his shiny smooth jaw and had a mad urge to taste it, to run her tongue over the slight dimple just above the strong, straight line of his chin.

"Nina." Intense relief and awed pleasure. His face broke into a dazzling grin. His hands came up, gesturing appreciation of the picture she made. "You look fantastic." He laughed. "I feel like I've been run over by a truck, you're so stunningly beautiful."

She laughed, too. He'd had the same impact on her.

"Even your hair...." He shook his head in wonderment.

"You preferred it long?"

"No...it's different, but it does suit you." Emphatically positive.

"I know you liked it long, but it got in the way with bending down to get hems right on dresses." She prattled, tingling with nervous excitement.

"Doesn't matter." His eyes said he adored her any way at all.

Nina's stomach curled. "You look great, too, Jack."

He took a deep breath. "May I come in, Nina?"

"Oh!" She expelled the breath she didn't know she'd been holding. She felt as skittish as a teenager on a first date, wanting everything to be perfect yet frightened of doing the wrong thing, going too far, not going far enough. It was silly. They'd had a baby, for heaven's sake, yet somehow the remembered intimacies made it worse. So much hung in the balance.

"I'm not going to jump you, Nina," Jack said softly. "I realise you need time."

He understood. Relief and pleasure coursed through her, resulting in a brilliant smile. "I'm glad you came, Jack." The words bubbled from her as she stood back and waved him in. "I'm sorry about last night, pushing you out so—so..."

"It's okay," he assured her. "It must have been a big strain, the baby, me, everything."

"Yes, it was. I didn't know what to think," she blurted.

"We'll work it out, Nina." His eyes were serious, wanting her agreement.

Her heart swelled with hope, and the love they had once shared shimmered through it. She wanted to throw herself at him, hug, kiss, make love with wild abandonment, revel uninhibitedly in the joy of being together again, of touching, feeling, knowing he was her man and she was his woman. She shut the door and forced herself to be sensible.

"I'd like that, Jack," she said with overwhelming sincerity.

The air between them was suddenly hypercharged with hopes, dreams and desires. Jack seemed to teeter forward on his toes, then rocked firmly back on his heels. His hands lifted towards her. He clapped them and said heartily, "Well, how's the kid been today?"

The kid.

It cleared Nina's mind of its heat haze, but she didn't take offence at the term this time. Jack meant well. He was trying. "Fine!" She smiled.

"She loved her bath. You should have seen her, Jack. It was so..."

Her throat seized up as the realisation hit her she was blathering on like a besotted mother who had no conversation bar her baby's trivial activities. It was one of Jack's criticisms of the effect of having children.

"Go on," he urged.

She swallowed. Her mind seized up. She couldn't think of anything bright to say. "You'll think I'm a vegetable." The words slipped out on a helpless sigh.

"Nina, I want to share everything with you. Don't shut me out." The anguished plea in his voice, in his eyes, tore at her heart.

"But you said..."

"Forget it. It doesn't apply to us."

She shook her head, unable to sweep the argument that had parted them under the carpet and pretend it never happened. "I don't want to bore you, Jack."

"You won't." He stepped forward, his hands lifting instinctively to her upper arms to press persuasion. "Seeing your face light up with joy, your eyes dance with delight—it could never bore me, Nina. I want to know what's behind the happy glow. I want it to spill over onto me. It's warm and wonderful and..." He expelled a long breath, and his thumbs fanned her flesh, wanting to draw her into him, enforced restraint allowing only a gentle caress. "Please don't hold back from me."

Her chest felt as tight as a drum, and her heart was playing percussion instruments on a wild scale. The desire in his eyes played havoc with any control she had, yet some thread of sanity wove through the swarm of feelings, reminding her what had triggered this passionate outpouring from Jack.

"You mean you want to hear about Charlotte's bath?"

"Yes. Anything. Everything," he replied vehemently.

She gave a nervous little laugh, her lashes sweeping down as a wave of self-consciousness increased her inner turmoil. "It's nothing, really," she dismissed in an agony of doubt.

"Nina, don't throw it away." A gentle finger tilted her chin, drawing her gaze to his. He smiled an appeal. "You always made such fun out of telling me what you'd been doing. Let me enjoy listening to you again."

She tried to relax, tried to respond, but it felt hopelessly flat now. It would sound forced and false. "I'm sorry, Jack. I've gone cold on it."

"Let me get you a drink." He released her and strode into the kitchenette, talking brightly, trying to coax her into being her old, natural self with him. "You used to keep sherry. Are you allowed a small tipple or do we stick to cups of tea? Tell me what you'd like."

"A small sherry wouldn't do any harm," she decided. "There's a bottle in the cupboard next to the fridge. Just a splash over lots of ice.'' She needed cooling down, too.

"Okay! Coming right up.''

She sank onto the stool on the other side of the kitchen counter, not offering to help, letting him find things himself, needing time to settle herself down and get a grip on what she should be doing. It was difficult not to simply feast her eyes on Jack, moving competently around, fixing them both drinks as though he was perfectly at home here. Except it might be different once she really introduced the baby into the equation, making it a test situation.

"How's that?'' he asked, placing a glass full of crushed ice tinted with amber sherry in front of her.

"Great! Thank you.''

"My pleasure. Now tell me what you fancy for dinner. I'm cooking tonight.''

Nina took a sip of her drink as she tried to formulate the best way of telling him their time together was curtailed.

"You just sit there and relax and I'll prepare everything,'' he went on, letting her know he was not going to crowd her.

"We're not going to have much time together, Jack. I have an appointment to fit a wedding dress in Sally's showroom at seven o'clock and I have to feed Charlotte before then. If you don't want to bother—''

"No, I'm not going to let you fall into bad eating habits.'' He shook his head at her in frowning concern and checked his watch. "Five forty-two. I can have a proper dinner cooked by six-thirty. What time do you usually feed the kid?"

"Six o'clock."

"How long does it take?"

"About twenty minutes."

"Then we should slot the meal in nicely before you have to go to work. I'll clean up afterwards." His face lit with inspiration. "You can leave the kid with me. Save any distraction while you work."

His off-the-cuff suggestion left Nina confounded. She had been winding herself up to test his attitude over minding the baby and he'd whipped the mat out from under her feet, so to speak. Her disbelief and confusion must have been written on her face. Assuming he was about to get a negative response, Jack instantly proceeded to argue his case.

"I am a responsible adult, Nina. You can safely leave the kid in my care. I promise if I'm worried about anything, I'll come to you. How does that sound?" he asked eagerly.

She was stunned. "I . . . well, if you think—"

"Trust me," he commanded, his green eyes boring directly into hers, unwavering in his sense of purpose, insistent that she accept his word.

Nina took a deep breath. Far be it from her to protest his offer or dampen his eagerness to please. The focus of his caring was still centred on her, but did that matter if it motivated him to spend time looking after Charlotte?

"All right," she agreed. "If you're sure you don't mind."

He grinned as though he'd won a lottery. "Glad to be of help." Vitality bubbled from him as he danced to the refrigerator, swinging its door open wide to peruse the contents. "How about a big, juicy steak?"

"A small one for me, please." She wasn't sure she could eat anything. Jack was not only taking over, he seemed to be turning everything around.

"Salad, jacket potatoes?"

"Yes," she agreed dizzily.

It was a relief to hear Charlotte's first tentative cry—something normal, expected, and no problem knowing what to do about it. "I'll have to leave you to it, Jack," Nina said quickly, slipping off the stool.

A louder, "Hey! Did you hear me?" cry told Jack where she was going. He swung around to catch her attention as she headed for the hall. "Are you, um, self-conscious about breast-feeding, Nina?" he asked somewhat diffidently. "I mean, would you mind bringing the kid out here so we can be together?"

Like a real family.

The thought zinged through Nina's mind, ballooning the hope, edging it with a silver lining. Her smile sparkled. "I'll be back in a few minutes."

His smile positively scintillated. "Great!"

Nina didn't exactly dance down the hall, but her heart certainly jigged. Once in the bedroom she swooped on the capsule, picking Charlotte up in mid-wail and twirling around with her. "Your daddy wants us with him," she whispered gleefully.

Charlotte returned an arch look and spluttered.

Nina laughed and carried her over to the change table, performing a swift nappy change as she wondered what to do about her own clothes. Her top would have to come off. Then she remembered the lovely silk Christian Dior dressing gown Jack had given her for her birthday over a year ago. Its dramatic black and white print wouldn't clash with her make-up. Besides, Jack would recognise it and feel pleased she was wearing it.

Nina could hardly believe how well everything was going. The tension of testing Jack was completely wiped out. When she returned to the living room, he fussed around, making sure she and the baby were comfortable in one of the armchairs, offering to fetch anything they needed and emitting all the pleasure of a proud dad as he watched Charlotte in action.

"This kid sure knows what it wants," he commented, a warm, appreciative gleam in his eyes.

Nina's stomach curled. Her breasts were highly sensitive at the moment. The tiny mouth sucking at her nipple sharply reminded her of many nights of love with Jack. Was he remembering, too?

The sense of intimacy being so strongly generated suddenly alerted Nina to the realisation it was still very early days in this new situation between them. "Tell me what's been happening to you, Jack," she invited quickly. "Your work and everything."

The conversation flowed smoothly enough, Jack very aware of keeping her at ease with him. The eight months of separation and the reason for it had to be laid to rest before they could really go forward. Nina couldn't be sure Jack's current attitude would last past the first flush of being together again. Charlotte would inevitably become more intrusive.

By the time Nina finished tending to Charlotte's needs and had changed back into her clothes, Jack had their meal ready. She carried the capsule out to the living room, setting it down near the cane lounge. Charlotte was still awake, happily crowing to herself, and Nina wanted to keep an eye on her, making sure it would be all right to leave her with Jack.

Surprisingly, Nina found she had a hearty appetite. She thoroughly enjoyed her dinner, relaxing in Jack's company while they ate. He even persuaded her into telling him about Charlotte's bath, chuckling at her description of the baby's initial stiffening at the touch of water and Nina's interpretations of the startled expressions on her face.

It was the kind of shared fun they used to have, and Nina was in buoyant spirits as she prepared to leave for her appointment. A last-minute check on Charlotte completely shattered her happy bubble of optimism. The tiny fists were clenched, and her face had the screwed-up air of concentration that Nina recognised only too well.

"Oh no! Not now," she groaned.

"What's wrong?"

"Charlotte is working up to dirtying her nappy. What am I going to do?" she wailed, frantically checking the time. "I can't be late. I'll have to come back and clean her up after I let Juliette in. If Charlotte starts crying—"

"Stop worrying." Jack gripped her shoulders to calm her agitation, and his eyes beamed confident assurance at her. "I'll take care of it. I trust I'll find everything I need in the bedroom? A clean nappy, baby oil, tissues, talcum powder?"

"Yes, but—"

"I can do it, Nina. Leave it to me. You go on and attend to business. Not a problem."

"You've never done anything like this, Jack," she cried, horrified at the idea of throwing him in at the deep end with a mess that would surely turn his stomach.

"Had a practice session this morning," he asserted. "I'm an expert."

"What?" Incredulity blitzed the horror.

"Maurice Larosa has a new baby son. That's why I was visiting the hospital. I got his wife to give me nappy-changing lessons," he said smugly. "I bet I can do it as good as you."

She shook her head dazedly. Jack taking nappy-changing lessons?

"Now, off you go." He good-humouredly turned her towards the connecting door to Sally's house. "I'll take charge here."

She went.

She wondered if Maurice's son had dirtied his nappy or simply wet it. There was a huge difference. Huge! As a test for having the intestinal fortitude for hands-on fatherhood, Charlotte was certainly supplying a hardliner. Nina had to acknowledge there was a terrible fascination in finding out if Jack could really handle it and still come up smiling.

CHAPTER TEN

JACK was curious. And intrigued. How did Nina know the kid was doing heavy business? He couldn't see any telltale signs. The baby bomb was looking up at him as placid as you please, big eyes widely alert as though reviewing the conversation it had heard and checking Jack out before accepting him as substitute minder.

"I'm your dad, kid," Jack advised. "Better get used to me."

The little face suddenly assumed a belligerent expression. The tiny arms stopped waving and straightened out, hands clenching.

"Want to fight, huh?"

No reply. A gathering of concentration on internal matters, eyes narrowing, face going red. Several seconds passed. It dawned on Jack that the kid was pushing. Then the job was done. Relief came. Relaxation. A look of blissful peace. Jack chuckled. It was so obvious.

"Good to get rid of that lot, eh?"

He recalled Nina's description of the range of expressions reflecting the kid's reaction to a bath and shook his head in amusement. Who would have thought personality was developed so young? He could see there might very well be a fascination in watching it grow. Maybe besotted parents weren't as foolish as he'd thought. On the other hand, it was patently ridiculous to let a pint-sized infant rule the roost.

He picked up the capsule and carried it into the bedroom. No point in lifting the kid out until he had to. Stuff might run down its legs. He put the capsule on the bed and examined what Nina had laid out on the change table. He figured a towel and a wet washer might be useful and fetched them from the bathroom. Nappy-changing carried unsuspected dangers. Maurice's kid had gone off like a fountain this morning, hitting him in the face before he could block the spray off with the absorbent pad.

Having assembled everything within easy reach, Jack felt supremely competent and confident as he gathered up the danger zone and moved it to the change table, holding the little body horizontally to prevent possible leakage. Mission successful. Jack grinned triumphantly as he unsnapped the fasteners on the terry-towelling body suit, freed the tiny feet from it, and pushed the garment up out of the operation area.

"Got to hand it to your old dad, kid. Think ahead. That's what you have to do in this life to avoid mishaps."

The response from her pursed lips was a spit-and-splutter raspberry.

"No respect," Jack chided. "You'll have to watch that, kid. I'm supposed to be the authority

in your life. You don't want to start off on the
wrong foot."

The odour started rising as Jack unfastened the
plastic tabs on the nappy. It was incredibly foul.
Worse than rotten egg gas. Jack's throat convulsed as he fought against gagging. Manfully he
peeled down the front section of the nappy. The
source of the smell revealed itself in all its slushy,
yellow-green horror.

"Yuk! No wonder you wanted to get rid of
that!"

A gurgle denoted agreement.

Jack hastily but carefully removed the liner that
contained most of the mess, burying it in a heap
of tissues. He set to work cleaning up the kid's
bottom. The stuff had oozed everywhere. Tissues,
he decided, were a great invention, but he was
glad he'd had the foresight to have a washer and
towel on hand to do a proper job of removing
every putrid smear.

The assault on his olfactory nerves lessened as
they got used to the stench. Or he got rid of it.
One way or another, it wasn't too revolting after
a while. Not the most pleasant of jobs, Jack reflected, but paint stripper wasn't pleasant, either,
and it was an unavoidable adjunct to his work
with furniture. Some things just had to be done.

He did, however, gain an insight into the fix-
ation parents had about potty-training. There was
definitely reason behind their madness. Cause
and effect. He appreciated how important—
indeed, obsessive—the issue could become when

a person was faced with this every day. Jack resolved to be more sympathetic to potty-training discussions in future.

"That does it," Jack informed the kid, having achieved absolute cleanliness.

He slid a fresh nappy under the pearly white bottom, positioning it with well-trained precision. A bit of baby oil, a shake of talcum powder, and all was sweetness and light. Gently moving the tiny legs apart in order to bring up the front piece of the pad, Jack was suddenly struck by the irrefutable fact he was looking straight at unfamiliar territory.

Maurice's kid had recognisable equipment. A boy was a boy. This was...a girl.

Jack blinked. Somehow she didn't look right. It took him a second or two to realise he'd never seen what a girl looked like before the age of puberty. No sisters. No girl cousins, either. Having been in a boys' boarding school from age seven, he simply hadn't been exposed to a young girl's anatomy.

Not that it changed, he reminded himself, but it obviously got more disguised. This was...so bare. It gave him a funny feeling—a strong rush of tenderness mixed with a fierce urge to protect.

A girl. A daughter...

Jack shook his head in bemusement. Was this what the father-daughter thing was about? A girl looked so vulnerable. She needed a dad to keep her safe from the bad guys. Mothers were fine. Mothers were irreplaceable, he amended, the memory of Nina breastfeeding still highly vivid and captivating. But fathers definitely had their role to play in looking after little kids.

"Don't you worry, Charlie girl," he told his daughter as he covered her up and fitted the nappy firmly with the tabs. "Any bad guy is going to have to get past me, and I'm no pushover."

She made a popping sound with her mouth.

"Blowing me a kiss, huh?" He grinned as he put her feet in the body suit and did up the press studs. "There you are. All snug. How about another kiss?" He gave her tummy a little tickle as he leaned over and made a popping sound with his lips.

She gazed at in him in wide-eyed fascination. Jack prompted her with a repeat demonstration. She caught on and gave it right back to him.

"That's Daddy's girl!"

He suddenly heard the drooling indulgence in his voice and jolted upright, appalled at how quickly, how insidiously he had been drawn into baby drivel. It was a highly sobering experience. Never in his worst nightmares had he imagined himself succumbing to such soppy nonsense.

He eyed the kid with glowering suspicion. There was a power here that had to be resisted. No kid was going to turn him into a blathering idiot. No, sir! He was master of his own behaviour.

"Back to your capsule, kid," he commanded, picking up the thimble-sized piece of dynamite and transporting it to the restricted area where it belonged, doing no harm and coming to no harm.

"A place for everything and everything in its place," Jack recited sternly, ignoring the wail of protest as he dealt with the mess on the change table.

The wailing continued. Jack set everything to rights in the bedroom, then carried the capsule out to the living room. There was still the cleaning up to do in the kitchen. The kid was demanding more attention. Jack recognised the conflict of interests and decided it had to be nipped in the bud.

"Listen up, kid," he addressed his demanding daughter in the voice of paternal authority. "You and I need to come to an accommodation."

It got through to her. She stopped wailing and gave him her attention.

"The human race rubs along best if people consider each other," Jack explained. "I'm not going to have your mother come back to dirty dishes in the sink. You've had your time quota from me. It's your mum's turn now. So quit being selfish."

A spit-and-splutter raspberry.

Jack wagged his finger at her. "No more lip from you, young lady. I'll put on some music. We can both listen to it while I do the work. That's it. Your dad has spoken."

A satisfactory silence followed this little homily. Jack hummed happily to himself as he selected the Beatles anthology album from Nina's collection and slid it into her disk player. Proper instruction and education. That was the trick, he decided. He turned the volume down low on the sound system, considering delicate eardrums, and started off Charlie girl's musical education with a gentle blast from the past.

"How's that, kid?" he asked on his way to the kitchenette.

No reply. Totally enthralled with the new experience.

Jack congratulated himself. He was wise to the baby game. Kids could dominate a relationship in no time flat. They looked helpless and cute, but they were really dyed-in-the-wool tyrants, given free rein. Things had to be kept in proportion. There had to be respect, discipline, an understanding of limits.

It was really quite simple to handle, once one appreciated the power game being played. As the old saying went, it was the hand that rocked the cradle that ruled the world. Anyone who let the kid in the cradle do the ruling was asking for trouble.

CHAPTER ELEVEN

"IT WILL be done first thing in the morning," Nina assured Juliette Hardwick for the umpteenth time, barely restraining herself from pushing the bride-to-be out the door.

"Don't worry, Juliette," Sally chimed in, having joined them to do her public relations priming of the client. Sally never missed a trick in delivering the dream. "I'll bring you the dress myself tomorrow evening. You'll look absolutely perfect on your wedding day."

"You don't think I've got too thin, do you?" came the anxious question.

More lingering, Nina thought in exasperation, desperately eager to get back to Jack and Charlotte. Jack must have coped somehow, since he hadn't come looking for assistance, but it could be pride holding him back. Nina was full of trepidation at what she would find when she returned to her flat.

Sally soothed and flattered, and finally Juliette bid them good night and left. The door had barely closed behind her when Sally grabbed Nina's arm, detaining her from dashing away on the instant. Her bright hazel eyes gleamed with the need to know.

"Obliging attitude?" she queried, her eye-brows waggling madly in the direction of the granny flat.

"He offered to mind Charlotte. I didn't have to ask." Nina rushed the words out.

"*Great* attitude!"

"He said he'd had nappy-changing practice." Incredulity was still bombarding her mind.

"*Fantastic* attitude!"

"And Charlotte was working up to dirtying her nappy when I left."

Sally laughed in delight. "That'll test him."

Nina was too concerned about the outcome to laugh. She pulled out of Sally's hold. "I've got to go. I'll collect the wedding dress in the morning."

"Don't forget the reward," Sally called after her and merrily started trilling her favourite song, Mendelssohn's "Wedding March".

Which was certainly jumping the gun, in Nina's opinion. Even if Jack had managed to get through tonight's testing ground without major damage to the attitude he'd adopted, it was only a start in the right direction. Nina couldn't blind herself to the consequences of making a wrong decision with him, no matter how much she wanted everything to turn out well.

Hope and desire were traps. When Jack was with her, Nina found it impossible not to re-spond to him. He tapped so many feelings in her it was all too easy to fall into those traps. If she wasn't careful, she'd find herself making excuses and compromises instead of facing up to realities.

A panicky tension gripped her as she reached the door to the flat. With her fingers grasping the handle, she paused and forced herself to take a long, deep breath. To appear in an emotional flap would give the wrong signals. Jack had asked her to trust him. She had to assume everything was fine.

She also had to watch out for signals herself, bring an objective view to the scene. Jack might try covering up his real thoughts and feelings about the baby for her sake, but they would come out in the end. No one could hide the truth forever, and once resentments could no longer be contained, they had the potential to explode with devastating effect.

Having cautioned and calmed herself as best she could, Nina turned the handle and started to open the door, keenly listening for the sound of trouble—a cry from Charlotte, a curse from Jack, a muttered imprecation against children in general and the twist of fate that had bedevilled his life plan.

Music. Nothing but music playing at a reasonable volume. Nina recognised one of the Beatles' songs. Not exactly a lullaby. Ringo's drumbeat was not in the somnolent category, more in the foot-tapping, hand-clapping class. Jack was very fond of the Beatles' music, but what of Charlotte?

Nina peered around the door, seeking some hint of what she was about to confront. Jack was sprawled in the cane armchair closest to the kitchenette and facing in her direction. He was half-hidden by the *Herald*, its large pages propped on his thighs and held up in front of him so Nina could only see his hair above them. Apparently he was engrossed in reading an article and hadn't heard the door open.

Charlotte's capsule lay on the floor between Jack's armchair and the lounge. Nina couldn't see over the raised end of it to check the baby, but concluded she must be asleep. There was not a peep out of her. A glance at the kitchen counter assured Nina Jack had cleaned up after their meal, as promised.

Relief washed through her. His relaxed air, Charlotte's silence, work all done, no evidence of any trauma—nothing for Nina to worry over. Relief was swiftly followed by pleasurable amazement. Jack's confidence in his competence was not misplaced. This was a better start than Nina could ever have credited, given the unpropitious circumstances.

Curious to see how well he had managed the nappy-change and reclothing Charlotte, Nina very quietly closed the door behind her and tiptoed forward. Her heart missed a beat when she saw that the capsule was empty.

"What have you done with Charlotte?" The question flew off her tongue, alarm rising rapidly and giving her voice a sharp edge.

The newspaper was instantly twitched down, Jack's face appearing above it, beaming surprised delight. "You're finished already. Everything go well?"

"Jack, where is Charlotte?" She gritted the words out, holding herself back from flying at him tooth and claw.

"Right here," he answered blithely, lowering the newspaper to his knees so she could see. "Just like a puppy," he said, smiling at the baby clinging like a limpet to his chest. Without any support whatsoever!

"A puppy?" Nina repeated, dazed, alarm subsiding into shock.

"You know how puppies snuggle up to their mother, hanging all over her. Or if she's left them alone, they go into a huddle, clutching onto each other," Jack expounded happily. "Must be the warmth or the comfort of another heartbeat."

"Right!" Nina agreed limply.

It was a strain, holding herself back from rushing forward and snatching Charlotte off his chest. She told herself Jack's arms were in a good position to halt Charlotte from rolling off him, and he was leaning back in the chair, so it wasn't likely she would flop backwards. Apart from which, Jack liked dogs. It was okay for him to compare Charlotte to a puppy. It was a good sign he was viewing her favourably. Fondly.

"Must be instinctive," he concluded.

It could be called bonding, Nina thought, trying to look on the bright side as she cast an eagle eye over her baby. Charlotte wasn't moving. The nappy bulge looked right. The press studs on the body suit were all matched up, fastened properly. Nothing was askew.

"How come you picked her up?" Nina asked, curious to know more of how Jack thought about their child. She hadn't expected him to bother with her beyond the necessary.

He gave a funny grimace. "She took a dislike to one of the songs and started yelling her disapproval. I tried telling her why she should appreciate it but she wouldn't listen until I got her up close to me."

"And then she fell asleep on you?"

Jack heaved a rueful sigh. "I think I must have bored her with musical technicalities. Or it was too much for her to take in. She *is* only little."

Nina giggled. She couldn't help it. Jack didn't have a clue how to handle Charlotte. First he had referred to her as *the kid*, trying for an impersonal distance. Then he reasoned she was like a puppy, to account for her need to be comforted when she cried. Talking to her as though she were a fellow adult did, however, take the cake. No way was a week-old baby going to understand a word of what he said.

Jack looked at her quizzically. "What's so funny?"

Nina quickly shook her head as she swallowed her laughter. "Hysterical relief," she explained, not wanting to put him off any effort to come to terms with the problem of having a child he didn't want. "I was a bit wound up, having left you with one of the worst aspects of taking care of a baby."

He shrugged. "No worse than stripping paint."

As he folded the newspaper to lay it aside, Nina bit her lips to stop the giggles erupting again. Jack's logic was certainly novel, but if it worked for him, she was not about to criticise or make fun of it. Any practical parallel he could find to keep his toleration level up was fine by her.

Having got rid of the newspaper, he placed a supporting hand around Charlotte's shoulders and head, his other hand cupping her bottom, and he leaned forward, plucking her from his chest. "Down you go, Charlie girl," he crooned, swooping her smoothly into the capsule. "Mummy's turn now," he added as he tucked the bunny rug around her.

"Turn?" Nina queried, bemused by Jack's indulgent manner with their daughter. He was even calling her by name now. At least, his version of her name.

He stood, grinning, a wicked gleam in his green eyes. "For a cuddle," he enlightened her, stepping forward purposefully.

Was he expecting, demanding a reward? Had he calculated what he had to do in order to get what he wanted? Turn and turnabout?

Tension zipped along Nina's nerves. *Control*, her mind screamed. She whipped up a hand to stop him. "I'm not a baby, Jack. I'm a woman."

"I know," he said warmly, taking her hand and putting it on his shoulder as he slid an arm around her waist. "I've got the music on. Let's dance."

Her body hit his and didn't want to leave it. Besides, dancing was relatively harmless, she argued, nothing more than a social convention, done in public all the time. Except she knew perfectly well Jack was a great dancer, a sexy dancer, and she was playing with fire. Heat was racing through her veins even before he gathered her closer.

"I need to hold you," he murmured, his mouth hovering near her ear, his breath tingling over her skin. The ache of yearning in his voice sent an echo reverberating through her body, stirring the need to be held, to feel his weight, his strength, his warmth, his sheer animal maleness.

"It's been so long," he groaned, his hands sliding over her back, relearning its curve, revelling in the sensual rub of silk on flesh, his and hers.

Yes, so long. The words moaned through her mind, wanting freedom of expression. It would be treacherously easy to close her eyes to the future and seize the moment, taking what she could while she could. Would that be so wrong when it felt this right to be held by Jack? But if it was so right, it would still be right tomorrow, she cautioned herself. And all the tomorrows that made up the future.

They swayed to the music. Tempted beyond caution, Nina slid both arms around Jack's neck, pressing her breasts against the satisfying solidity of his chest, loving the firm delineation of his muscles as he sucked in a quick breath, then slowly released it.

It was dangerously wanton of her. She knew it but didn't care. She had been too long apart from him, too long feeling only half alive. Her body was singing at every brush with his, exulting in the moving pressure of his thighs, arching sensuously to the moulding of his hands. She felt the growing hardness of his arousal, and excitement speared through her, leaving a shivery weakness that forcefully reminded her she wasn't ready for this.

A paralysing thought crashed into her mind and stopped her feet dead. "Jack..."

"Natural response," he soothed.

"Jack, have you been with other women?"

He met her gaze with sizzling sincerity. "Not since you, Nina. I don't want any other woman."

"Oh!" She flushed at his directness, at the desire blazing from him, searing her conscience with doubts about her decision to go her own way and leave him to his.

"You're the only woman I've ever loved. The only person I've ever loved, Nina," he said huskily.

Her heart turned over. Jack was like her, alone in the world, no family to speak of, and though friends were good, it wasn't the same as loving and knowing yourself loved. Without thought, without reason, Nina's whole being surged to meet him as he bent his head to kiss her.

Their mouths melded, emotional intensity swiftly moving to a passionate expression of their craving to be one again. It was only when Jack scooped her into a more intimate fit with his erection, wildly accelerating the need to merge together, that Nina's swimming senses whirled back to some common sense.

"Jack!" she gasped, tearing her mouth from his, her hands scrabbling to hold his head back. She choked out the words in incoherent little bursts. "I can't. The birth. I'm sorry. I'm not— I didn't mean . . ."

"Not fit yet," Jack interpreted, sighing raggedly as he eased away and met her frantic eyes with rueful understanding. He stroked her cheek, transmitting tender caring as he smiled, warm pleasure welling over desire. "It's enough to know you feel the same, Nina."

"I have an appointment for a medical checkup next week," she babbled, not realising she was implying a promise, rushing to excuse the frustration of not following through on the promise she had recklessly implied in flying with her instincts here and now.

"It doesn't matter. I don't care how long we have to wait. What's another week or a month?" His smile spread into a happy grin. "I'm already on top of the world knowing you want me as much as I want you."

Her heart stopped its mad beating, hanging suspended for a mind-blowing second. She'd done it! Committed herself without thinking! Only to making love with him, she feverishly excused. Her pulse picked up again, drumming through her temples, definitely a rush of blood to the head. And other parts of her anatomy.

Jack planted a gentle kiss on her forehead. "I promise I'll keep it cool until the doctor says it's okay. I wouldn't hurt you for anything, Nina."

Cool, yes. Better to stay cool for as long as she could. Though it would be wrong to lead Jack on and not deliver. If she just took one step at a time... The big risk was in taking too much for granted.

Jack tilted her face up to his, his eyes probing hers with compassionate concern. "Was the birth very rough on you, Nina?" he asked softly.

She grimaced. "There was a clock on the wall. I kept telling myself if I survived one more minute I might make it through actually having the baby."

"That bad," he muttered, distressed by the description. "I wish I'd been with you."

"It's behind me, Jack. I've got Charlotte now, and she's worth far more than one day's pain to me." Needing him to realise and appreciate the importance she placed on their daughter, she added, "She was going to be my world. She'll always be an essential part of it. If you hurt her, you hurt me."

He looked taken aback. "I'd never hurt a kid, Nina. What on earth gave you that idea? I know I said kids were..." He hesitated over what words to choose.

"An abomination," she finished dryly.

"Well, they can be," Jack quickly qualified, "but the way I see it, that's more often the fault of the parents. Kids need a bit of firm direction now and then or they just run wild. Which isn't good for anybody."

Nina couldn't argue with that reasoning. She agreed with it. Though the word *firm* needed discussion.

"Anyway," Jack went on, "Charlie girl and I are getting along fine. Don't be worrying about things I said, Nina. I'll be a better dad than most."

He spoke so earnestly, Nina let the subject slide. Picking at old wounds didn't do any good. Besides, he'd certainly displayed a promising attitude. She smiled. "Thank you for looking after her so well tonight, Jack."

He grinned, relieved that she had accepted his efforts to deliver peace of mind on favourable paternal attributes. "I've been more than rewarded," he said magnanimously.

The idea of reward again. It struck a false note with Nina. She didn't like it. Not one bit. Sally might advocate a system of rewards as eminently workable, but Nina didn't want her relationship with Jack to work that way. She wanted him to care for Charlotte because she was a much-loved daughter, not because he might be rewarded with a session of lovemaking with the woman who happened to be Charlotte's mother.

It preyed on Nina's mind long after Jack left that night. Love wasn't based on manipulation. Love, to her mind, was a natural reaching out to each other, an open and honest expression of genuine feeling. To reduce it to a bargaining counter or a stick-and-carrot manoeuvre was anathema to her.

She did not doubt Jack loved her. Everything he did and said reflected it. But if he couldn't come to love Charlotte... A deep sadness dragged at her heart. Their baby, their child.

She had to tell him, lay it on the line what it meant to her and why. If he understood where she was coming from, would it help? Would it make the difference?

A sense of futility washed through her. Impossible to force what wasn't felt. Not all the words in the world could achieve that. The only realistic course was to wait and see.

CHAPTER TWELVE

"TONIGHT is the night, Spike," Jack informed his dog, who stood in the bathroom doorway, watching him shave.

Spike settled down on his haunches, rested his big shaggy head on his front paws and closed his eyes. He'd heard the same words all day. Clearly they excited his master, but since nothing new had happened, there seemed no point in responding until a change did occur. This shaving business every afternoon was no longer new.

"Sleep if you like, but I won't be sleeping. No, sir. Not if the doctor gives the okay. Good thing it's Friday. Maybe Nina will let me stay over the weekend."

Spike opened an eye. The tone of voice was different.

"Don't worry. I'll come back and feed you. Bring Nina and the kid with me. She's not a bad little kid, Spike. Good as gold. You'll like her."

A querying whine seemed appropriate.

Jack grinned at him. "You can learn to play dad, too. Look after her as you would a puppy. Keep her in check, give her a lick, warn off the bad guys."

The last words were growled, so Spike growled in agreement.

Jack laughed, unable to contain his high spirits. Cautioning himself with the possibility that Nina might need more recovery time made no difference to the tingle of anticipation. If that were the case, well, he'd take it on the chin and rise to the occasion. Or not rise, he corrected himself, instructing his anatomy to behave in an appropriate manner. Love came first, desire second.

But he sure hoped everything was fine. Celibacy did not suit him. His sex drive had been in overdrive ever since he had sighted Nina again. Being with her so much over the past couple of weeks had exercised his powers of restraint to the limit. Nevertheless, he'd hold off like a gentleman as long as he had to. Nina needed cossetting. She'd been through a bad time.

Jack put down the razor, splashed water over his face, towelled off, then closely examined the result of his shave in the bathroom mirror, running his hand over the shiny, smooth skin. Not a trace of stubble anywhere. Satisfied, he opened the new bottle of aftershave lotion and dabbed it on. Obsession by Calvin Klein. Cost him over seventy dollars.

Spike stirred, leaped to his feet. He sniffed the air and barked.

Jack grinned at him. "You like it, Spike?"

A yelp of agreement.

"Appealing. That's what the salesgirl said. I wonder if appealing means sexy? What do you think, Spike? Does this smell sexy?"

Spike's howl sounded like a mating call.

It put Jack in a great mood for getting dressed and on his way. New clothes, too. Casual smart. The open-necked olive green shirt had a nice feel to it, soft and silky. The snugly fitting fawn trousers didn't need a belt. The less obstacles to undressing, the better, Jack figured. Fumbling did not feature in his plans for tonight.

It would also be good if Charlie girl cooperated by sleeping through as many hours as she could. Give Nina a real break so she could relax and not worry about interruptions and hurrying things. All going well on the medical side, he'd have to speak to Charlie girl about considering her mother's needs. Her father's needs, as well. He rehearsed a few lines as he slid on a pair of leather moccasins that didn't require socks.

"Listen up, kid. You and I need to come to an accommodation. Give your mum a good rest tonight, and tomorrow I'll introduce you to my dog. How's that, Spike?"

A bark of approval.

"We'll be having a few changes around here soon, Spike. I've got myself a family. Well, almost. Nina's holding out on marrying me, but I'm sticking in there, and sooner or later she'll say yes."

He bent to give his faithful companion a good ruffle behind the ears. "Happy days are coming, Spike. We might even get a little dog for you to boss around and lick into shape for Charlie girl. You are a bit big for her."

The growl could have been pleasure from the scratching, but Jack saw a doubtful gleam in the beady brown eyes.

"You're right. I'm big, too. The trick is to be gentle with her. No rough stuff. Okay?"

Spike nodded.

"Good dog. Come on. It's early dinner again for you, but I got a great bone from the butcher to make up for it. Lots of meat left on it."

Bone was the magical word. Spike perked up and pranced towards the staircase, his great bushy tail swishing with eagerness. Jack was just as eager as his dog. They raced down the stairs together, barking and laughing.

Once in the kitchen, Jack wasted no time in handing over the special treat. Spike growled his delight and approval and retreated to his corner to gloat over it. Hours of gourmet pleasure in this bone. He watched his water dish being filled and was content. This man was definitely the best of all possible friends. He even smelled good.

"Well, Spike," he said, "I'm off now. Wish me luck."

Having been given his heart's delight, Spike howled encouragement.

"Right on, Spike. Tonight could be the night."

CHAPTER THIRTEEN

NINA settled Charlotte for the night, fussing with the bunny rug, delaying the moment when she'd have to face Jack alone with no more responsibilities to claim her attention. At least, not for hours. It was only ten-thirty. Sometimes Charlotte slept through until almost three o'clock.

It wasn't as though she didn't want to make love with him, and the doctor had assured her there was no reason to hold back, yet a host of inhibitions were crowding her mind and playing havoc with her nerves, making her tense and apprehensive. She simply couldn't put aside the fact that it wasn't the same as it had been before she fell pregnant with Charlotte.

She wasn't carefree. She didn't have only herself to consider. Most of all, she was afraid that having sex wouldn't feel as satisfying as it should, either to her or to Jack. Giving birth to a baby had to have caused some physical difference, and if making love was a disaster, it would be awful.

As she straightened up from Charlotte's capsule she flashed a smile at Jack, who had accompanied her into the bedroom, ostensibly to say good night to his daughter. "I have to go to the bathroom. Won't be long."

She fled before he could say anything, shutting herself in the bathroom like a panic-stricken virgin. It was ridiculous. Jack had been so patient, understanding, kind and thoughtful. She loved him. And tonight he was so excitingly attractive she'd barely been able to eat any dinner. Her stomach kept curling. Even the smell of his aftershave lotion had a tantalising appeal.

Aware that she was slightly sticky from breast-feeding, Nina whipped off her dressing gown and panties and stepped under the shower. Perhaps a warm spray all over would help her relax. Feeling freshly clean was an appealing idea, too, although she had showered before Jack's arrival this evening.

Her breasts weren't so tight since Charlotte had taken her fill. They weren't a worry. Fortunately, her skin was not disfigured by stretch marks, although she hadn't regained good muscle tone yet. The flesh on her abdomen felt slightly loose to her. Would Jack notice? It shouldn't matter, she sternly told herself. All in all, she was in good shape.

Except for the stretching inside. There was surely some. Her internal muscles had to be fairly elastic to have coped with a baby's passage, but Nina doubted they were as good as new again. What if she was, well, spongy? She wished Sally had had children. She could have asked her about it. Her doctor had said there was nothing to worry about, but he was a man. It was times like these when a woman needed a mother who cared enough to have an intimate discussion with her daughter.

Nina sighed and turned off the taps. She vowed to be on hand when Charlotte grew up and had a baby. Her daughter was not going to lack a sympathetic female ear, nor the loving reassurance a mother could give. There were many problems in being a woman. Many pleasures, too.

As she towelled herself dry, Nina concentrated on the pleasures. She didn't want to spend the rest of her life in a sexual vacuum. Jack was a great lover. Impossible to imagine anyone better. He really cared about making her feel good, and he knew how to do it.

Whether he turned into a loving father to Charlotte or not, Nina reasoned she owed it to herself to extend the loving experience with Jack, as long as he wasn't stirring up tensions and problems with their child. Tonight was the night. If she didn't jump this self-conscious barrier about her body, it was only going to get bigger and bigger in her mind. Maybe she should suggest dancing. Jack had a very seductive way of making her forget things when he danced with her.

Nina slid on the Christian Dior dressing gown again. She looked at her panties and decided no. She was going to do it. Make love with Jack, no matter what. Barriers were out. She moved over to the vanity bench and slid open the mirror cabinet above it. She took out the tiny bottle of perfume Sally had given her the morning after Charlotte was born, saying it was to remind her she was still a woman, as well as a mother.

Spellbound, by Estee Lauder. She dabbed some on her pulse points. It had a sexy scent. Definitely sexy. Jack would certainly get the message. No backing off tonight.

Nina returned the bottle to the shelf, slid the mirror door shut, took a deep breath and left the bathroom on a wave of unshakable determination and a waft of telling perfume. She heard Jack's voice in the bedroom. Without hesitation she went to join him.

"That's it, Charlie girl," he was saying as she walked in, his voice low and intense.

"What's it?" Nina asked curiously. Jack had a weird way of talking to Charlotte, as though she understood everything he said. Nina sometimes wondered if it was a subconscious defence against his dislike of babies. If he spoke to Charlotte as though she were an adult, she wasn't *one of them*.

He straightened up and swung to face her, a satisfied little smile hovering on his lips. "Oh, I was just telling her about my dog."

A light switched on in Nina's mind. Jack spoke to his dog as though it understood everything, too. She'd found it rather endearing, although it only minimally reduced her unease with the huge, intimidating animal. Jack had said Charlotte was like a puppy. Since he loved his dog, maybe it was best he kept likening Charlotte to a puppy.

"That's nice," she said. Or was she going stark, raving mad in her need to have everything turn out right?

"She's going to sleep now," Jack assured her as he left Charlotte's side. "Are you okay?" His eyes raked hers, checking for any sign of reluctance, assuring himself there was no last-minute change in the current of aroused sexuality that had been flowing so strongly between them all evening.

"Yes." Unmitigated consent, throbbing through her, reaching out to him, pulling him to her in wanton dismissal of the cares that had trip-wired the churning desire to know and feel every dimension of intimacy with this man.

The cautious query in his eyes winked out. A few strides and she was in his arms, no hesitation, an urgent claiming that couldn't wait any longer to savour the freedom to sate their senses in each other. For several seconds he simply held her crushed to him, as though soaking in the imprint of her body.

"You feel so good." His cheek rubbed over her hair as he swayed, rocking with an exultation of spirit that swirled through her, setting her heart pounding with anticipation. He inhaled deeply, the air suddenly sweeter to him than ever before. "Smell so good," he added with a raw sigh.

"You, too," she whispered.

"I'm dying to taste all of you, Nina."

"Yes." A hiss of elation, wild recklessness seizing her.

Her arms locked around his neck, and she
arched against him, revelling in the tension of his
hard, hot muscles as she tilted her head back, her
eyes a dark, sultry invitation, her lips already
parted for him. She needed to be swept into a
fast and furious maelstrom of passion, needed
to have sensation bombarding her mind, needed
to feel, not think, and for the feeling to be so
intense, so pervasive, so exciting, there wasn't
room for anything else, only Jack and her, man
and woman, fusing in a feast of feeling.

She met his mouth eagerly in a kiss of urgent
hunger, their tongues dancing with wildly erotic
intent, dipping deeply, sweeping, darting,
thrusting, coiling around each other in a tantalising tango, driving towards the ultimate
coupling, a feverish forerunner fuelling their
desire for fulfilment. She moved her hips pro-
vocatively against his, and his hands swept down
to her buttocks to incite a more raunchy rolling
contact, aggressive and fiercely possessive.

It was intensely exciting.

Jack tore his mouth from hers, groaning with
pre-climax tension. "This is too fast."

"Not for me," Nina said, wanting to lose
herself in the throes of passion.

He swung her over to the bed and wrenched
her gown open. In hot haste he swept the silk
from her arms, his hands quickly scooping up to
cup her breasts tenderly, weighing them as though
they were newly precious to him.

"The magic of a woman," he said huskily, and
bent to curl his tongue around her distended aur-
eoles, sending piercing shafts of pleasure through
Nina, totally immobilising her for several enthralling moments before the need to touch him
snapped her into movement.

She dragged his shirt out of his trousers. It was
all the prompt he needed to break off his absorption in her to discard his clothes. Their eyes
shone with rapturous delight in each other, and
their hands revelled in the blissful sensuality of
skin against skin, fingers grazing, luxuriating in
touch, warm flesh seething with sensation.

"I never stopped remembering you," Nina
whispered, "but feeling makes it real."

"Let me make it lastingly real, Nina."

He clamped her naked body to his as he carried
her with him onto the bed, then beguiled her with
a shower of kisses that sucked and caressed,
teased and ravished. She writhed voluptuously
under the smouldering heat of his lips and
tongue, uninhibitedly offering him the freedom
to do all he wanted. Her breasts tingled. Her
stomach rippled with spasms of excitement. Her
thighs quivered. Then the sweet ecstasy of the
most intimate of all kisses drove her mindless with
need for the exquisite feeling of him filling her.

She raked his shoulders in frantic urging.
"Come into me now, Jack. Now," she cried.

He surged over her, into her, and she wound
her legs around him, lifting herself to the fast,
beautiful, slide of his flesh, the glorious strength

and power of it pulsing forward, crowding the waiting emptiness, taking it by storm, injecting an explosion of sensation that held her on a pinnacle of pure bliss.

"Again," she begged.

The sheer poignant splendour of it held her impaled as the thrust was repeated and repeated in the vibrant rhythm of intense possession, transporting them both into the inner world of oneness, where neither had any existence without the other and desire was answered and satisfied in the wild, orgasmic heat of giving and taking.

Wave after wave of exquisite delight convulsed Nina's body, overriding the memories, turning dreams into the vibrant substance of a reality that was beyond imagination. Love had so many forms, but this was the heart and soul and body of it, this union that communed with instinct, rejoicing in its sublime rightness. On one final crest of ecstasy she felt the added spill of Jack's climax, like hot foam rushing to mingle with the swirl of her sweet release, and her arms curled around him, bringing him down to her to kiss once more in a seal of completion.

Her man, the only one who had ever made her feel this incredible sense of fragility and strength, both vulnerable and invincible, stirring her trust in him to let herself go and exult in a togetherness that went beyond anything earthly. There was awe and wonder in their kiss, a celebration of love fulfilled, their lips tingling deliciously as they drew apart.

"Jack . . ." She breathed his name with a sigh of blissful happiness, hugging him tightly to her.

"You and me, Nina," he murmured, wrapping her in his arms and carrying her with him as he eased his weight off her and rolled onto his back. "Nothing could ever be as great as this," he concluded, his contentment settling around her like a warm cloak of lovely security.

"It was all right for you, then?" she asked, not really needing the assurance but wanting to hear it.

He laughed, a deep rumble of pleasure. "Nothing in the world could be more right, my love."

She smiled. "It was great for me, too."

For a while they simply luxuriated in lying together. Nina loved rubbing her legs against Jack's powerfully muscled thighs and calves. He had such a magnificent physique. His broad chest rose and fell under her cheek in a quiet hum of happiness. She played her finger pads teasingly over the erotic places she knew, just under his hipbone, down the side of his rib cage, near his groin, enjoying the spasmic shiver of pleasure she aroused.

Jack ran his fingernails over her back, lightly raking her skin. It made her feel like purring. She adored it. He could do it for hours, and she'd love every minute of it. Being naked with Jack was a hedonistic delight, packed with a multitude of sensory pleasures.

"I like your aftershave lotion," she said.

"It's called Obsession." She heard his grin. "I very much want you obsessed with me."

She laughed. "I am. My perfume is called Spellbound."

"Ah! You have me entranced."

"Mmm..." She snuggled languorously, indulging herself in stretching and curling over him, so delectably different to being coldly alone. "I could stay like this forever," she murmured.

"Well, it would be a step in the right direction if you married me." Jack rolled the words out confidently.

She wanted to. But... "It's not that easy, Jack," she said regretfully.

"We can make it easy, Nina. We just get Sally to arrange everything. I'll happily pay her fee, so it's no trouble to you."

"I didn't mean the business of making arrangements."

"What then?" He turned her onto her back and heaved himself onto his side so he could look into her eyes and watch the play of expression on her face. "Tell me the problem, Nina," he gently insisted.

There was no avoiding the truth, and she didn't want to. Honesty was the only way to go in this open intimacy between them. She had to hope Jack would understand, and she trusted he would appreciate where she was coming from.

"It goes back a long way, Jack," she said ruefully.

"I'm listening."

She held nothing back, telling him about her childhood, her parents' constant bickering, their resentments at being trapped by the responsibility of looking after the child neither of them had wanted, her hatred of asking them for anything, the misery of slinking away from arguments, making herself as unobtrusive as possible, the lonely sense of not really belonging anywhere, her grandmother's attitude of paying for her keep when she went to live with her after the divorce.

The memory of her mother's and grandmother's attitudes did not concern Nina so much. She knew she would do her utmost never to load her daughter with negative feelings. It was the memory of all the hurtful rejections from her father that weighed on her heart.

"My dad always found me a nuisance, Jack. Everything he ever did for me was a chore. He looked at me as though I were a constant irritation. It made me shrink inside."

"Did he hit you, Nina?" Jack asked softly.

"No more than the occasional smack. It wasn't physical abuse, Jack. It was his attitude towards me that hurt. He simply didn't want me in his life."

"He shouldn't have married your mother. Bad decision. You would have been better off adopted by a couple who wanted a baby, Nina."

She took a deep breath. He wasn't applying what she was saying to himself. She had to bring it home to him. "Jack, you didn't want a baby, either."

He frowned, not liking the parallel she was drawing. "You think I'd act like that with our daughter?"

"I don't want Charlotte to ever feel what I felt, Jack," she said earnestly. "I know you mean well, and you've been very good with her, but I'm afraid you won't be able to keep it up."

He pondered that for a while, his eyes sad and sympathetic as they scanned hers, taking in the doubts they harboured. "I really dug my grave with my mouth, didn't I?" he remarked wryly.

Nina was relieved to see he wasn't offended. She reached up and stroked his cheek. "I love you, Jack. You're a wonderful person. I don't want to drag you into parenthood if it doesn't suit you. It would end up hurting all of us."

He nodded. "I see what you mean, but I honestly don't think you have a lot to be afraid of with me, Nina. I can't promise you I won't make mistakes. This is new territory for me."

"For both of us," she acknowledged fairly.

He placed a gentle finger on her lips. His eyes pleaded for her belief. "I can promise you I'll never knowingly make our kid feel she isn't wanted or doesn't belong. I've been through that myself. I sure as hell wouldn't do it to my own kid."

His sincerity was beyond doubt. Nina recollected what he'd said about nannies and the alienation from home life by being sent to boarding school at a young age.

"Don't you worry," he went on strongly. "Charlie girl is going to have a very special place in our lives. She'll know it, too. Look at Spike."

This last comment threw Nina. "What has our daughter got to do with your dog?"

"When I took him home from the animal shelter he was a cowed and beaten dog. Whoever his previous owner was had woefully mistreated him. Broken his spirit. I gave Spike confidence in himself. Now he thinks he owns the place," Jack declared, proving his capability of restoring faith in a dog.

Nina couldn't help smiling. "Charlotte isn't a puppy, Jack. Human beings are a bit more complex."

He gave her a wise look. "Maybe human beings make things complex when they should be kept simple."

"Maybe. In any event, let's give it some time. There's no need for us to rush into marriage."

His sigh carried reluctant resignation. "Living apart doesn't give me the best chance to prove I can be a good dad, Nina," he pointed out.

That was true, yet she couldn't bring herself to make a commitment she wasn't absolutely sure of. "Be patient with me, Jack," she pleaded. "I've seen my parents go through the marry in haste, repent at leisure experience. I don't want to be rushed."

"Fair enough," he agreed, kissing her lightly to show there were no hard feelings. He followed it up with a dazzling smile. "How about you and our daughter spending the weekend at my place? It lets me be a full-time dad for two days so you can judge how I'm doing," he added persuasively.

Jack's emphasis on the words *our daughter* was not lost on Nina. It would be an even better sign if he called her Charlotte, but Nina was content with one step forward at a time.

"Fair enough," she agreed happily, reaching to pull his head to hers again and turning to feel the warm, wonderful length of his body against hers.

Jack needed no further invitation to resume lovemaking, and Nina revelled in every exquisite nuance of their intimacy.

One barrier gone, she thought exultantly.

She fiercely hoped Jack could remove the other.

CHAPTER FOURTEEN

JACK learnt a highly sobering lesson the next morning. When it came to babies, triumph could be turned into disaster in no time flat.

There he was, thinking he'd achieved a great step forward. Charlie girl had slept right through the night, as her dad had tactfully suggested, giving her mum a good rest, not to mention the freedom to reacquaint herself with the highly pleasurable satisfaction of lovemaking between a man and a woman. A splendid kid, Jack had thought, one who knew the meaning of artful cooperation and followed it to the letter.

Then what happened? Because Charlie girl hadn't woken for her regular feed in the wee hours of the morning, when she had called for it at the respectable time of sunrise, Nina's breasts were so tight with milk, at the first bit of sucking it ran down the kid's throat like the gush of a tap having been turned on full blast. Too much to cope with. She'd choked and spewed everywhere, distressing Nina and not feeling too good herself.

Jack could not have imagined such a little kid being a projectile vomiter. He took over the cleaning-up detail, relieving Nina of that mess. And he certainly had to admire Nina's fast thinking. She figured out if she lay on her back and the kid had to suck up from her breasts, the flow wouldn't be such dynamite.

It solved the feeding problem. Unfortunately, a baby's stomach was only so big. It couldn't take the double helping of milk Nina's inbuilt maternal machinery had manufactured and stockpiled. Her breasts were still uncomfortably tight after the kid had filled up.

"I'll have to use a breast pump, Jack," she said worriedly. "Will you find a chemist shop and buy one for me, please?"

"A breast pump," he repeated, incredulously thinking of the sucking contraptions stuck onto cows' teats for milking. When he was in primary school he'd gone to a dairy farm on an education excursion and seen them in operation. Nina had to use something like that? The idea horrified him.

"Yes. I guess I should have had one on hand, but I didn't expect Charlotte to start sleeping through the night this soon."

Guilt writhed through Jack.

"I think there's a twenty-four-hour chemist shop at Epping if you wouldn't mind going for me," Nina urged.

"Of course, I'll go." He checked his watch. It was almost seven o'clock, too early for normal business hours. They were only a couple of streets away from Epping Road. "Should be back in about twenty minutes or so. Will you be all right, Nina?" he asked anxiously.

"Yes. I'll get you some money."

"No. I'll pay." Apart from his desire to look after her, this dreadful outcome was his fault. "Take care now. I'll be as fast as I can."

"Thanks for helping, Jack."

"Only too glad to."

It was the truth. He'd bungled badly. Nina was right. Human beings were more complex than he'd thought. As he raced out to the Range Rover and hit the road, he castigated himself for not even realising the dire consequences ensuing from his initiative with Charlie girl. And the poor little kid—she couldn't have realised, either. She'd trusted her dad and almost ended up drowning in her mother's milk.

It was like the environment, Jack thought. If one little part of the pattern was changed, it set up a chain reaction that messed up everything. Big mistake! It was just as well Nina didn't know about his father-to-daughter chat. He'd have a black mark against him.

She'd probably see it as selfish, cutting down on the kid's needs to have more time with her. Which was true, in a way. But he hadn't meant any harm. It was a salutory lesson. He'd be a lot wiser in the future about how he arranged things.

Luckily it was Saturday morning, and the traffic was light on Epping Road at this early hour. He made good time to the shopping centre. He found the all-night chemist and rang the bell for attention. A guy came to let him in, and Jack spelled out the problem. He was mightily relieved when the breast pump turned out to be relatively small with an easy-to-use hand pump attached to a suction cup and a little bottle.

"I'd recommend you buy a jar of wool fat, too," the pharamacist advised.

Jack's mind leapt from cows to sheep. "What for?" he asked warily.

"Your wife could get sore nipples from the breast pump. They're probably sensitive anyway. If they crack it'll be very painful for her. Wool fat's the best to use on them."

Cracked nipples! Things were going from bad to worse. Huge mistake!

"Right! I'll take a jar," Jack said quickly. "Anything else we might need?"

"No. She should be right if she takes care. If not, see a doctor."

"I'll see she takes every care," Jack vowed, hating the idea that any action of his would result in Nina having to see a doctor.

Nothing was simple, he decided, paying over the money and collecting the goods. Babies could really complicate the normal run of life. He'd observed this with his friends without fully appreciating how complicated it could become. He'd always thought control was the key to keeping the little monst—uh, moppets in their place, but it was now clear that control was a very tricky business. He'd have to give it more thought, more care.

Having climbed into the Range Rover, he set off for Lane Cove, determined to get on top of the baby game. No more finagling without knowledge of possible repercussions. He couldn't afford to let Nina catch him out on too many mistakes. After last night, he was certain the door was well and truly open for him. He wasn't about to shut it in his own face.

At least he had the whole weekend to make up for this mishap. If he ever met those parents of hers, he'd have a few things to say to them. Fancy not wanting Nina, giving her a hard time. He was lucky his own parents had only ignored him for the most part. Nina had had it much rougher than he had. No wonder she needed a lot of reassurance.

As for Charlie girl, Jack figured he had no problem there. She was a good kid. Listened to her dad like a little trooper. He'd have to find some private time to have a quick word with her today, tell her there was a new plan and she'd better get back to her normal schedule. They'd upset the applecart.

Tonight . . . well, maybe he'd just cuddle Nina.

Unless she wanted more than that.

In which case, he'd oblige.

He might very well take obliging to a new art form. The pharmacist had assumed Nina was his wife. Jack was going to turn that into a reality as soon as he could. It surely wouldn't take long for Nina to see he wasn't like her father. He wasn't like his father, either.

All it would take was some mutual understanding with Charlie girl. *She* recognised a good deal when she was handed one. Kids knew instinctively which side their bread was buttered on. It was simple mathematics. A girl needed a dad, and he was obviously the right one to have.

Jack fiercely hoped it *was* simple.

CHAPTER FIFTEEN

SOMETHING was badly wrong, and Nina couldn't ignore it any longer. It was getting worse, not better. Much worse. Ever since the first night Charlotte had slept through, her breasts hadn't felt right. This morning, both feeding times had been pure agony.

Over the past week she'd used the pump to drain off the excess milk. It hurt, but she'd persisted with it until yesterday. Maybe her inexperience was at fault there. Whatever the reason, her breasts now had a hard, hot, red lump towards her armpits and were extremely painful. She was definitely running a temperature. On top of which, Charlotte was fretful, as though she wasn't getting enough.

It hurt to lift the capsule. Nina realised she wouldn't be able to manage getting to her doctor on her own. Her head was in a swoon from the fever. It could be dangerous if she fainted. She took the most sensible course and rang Sally, who was close at hand and wouldn't mind doing her a favour.

"It's Nina," she announced quickly, cutting through Sally's customary greeting spiel. "I'm not well. I need your help."

"Be right there."

Nina put the receiver down with a grateful sigh. Sally never blathered on when action was required. She had a mind like a razor blade underneath her glittering sales persona. Within seconds she was at the connecting door, and she burst into the flat in a blaze of efficient purpose.

Nina turned groggily from the kitchen counter on which she had leaned to use the telephone. Sally took one look at her, grabbed hold and supported her over to the closest armchair. She clamped a hand on Nina's forehead and started questioning.

"Flu? Gastric? What?"

Nina haltingly explained what was wrong.

"Mastitis," Sally diagnosed. "Infection in your breasts. Might even be abscesses. My sister had the same problem. It can happen when you're weaning a baby."

"But I'm not weaning Charlotte," Nina wailed.

"She's sleeping through. Same thing. You'll need antibiotics to knock out the infection. Maybe pills to stop producing any more milk. Best to get you to your doctor right now."

Tears welled into Nina's eyes. "You mean I won't be able to feed Charlotte any more?"

"Depends on how bad the infection is. Babies do survive on bottles, Nina. This is no time to quibble about what's best for them. We've got to do what's best for you."

Nina felt too weak and upset to resist as Sally moved into top organisation mode, calling her secretary, who arrived pronto with Sally's handbag and car keys. Instructions were given to take business calls on the mobile telephone. The secretary was to stay in Nina's flat and look after the baby. If any problem arose, Sally could be reached on her car phone or at the doctor's surgery. Within minutes they were on their way.

"Does Jack know about this?" Sally asked.

"No."

"You didn't tell him you were having problems?"

"I didn't want to worry him."

The tears gathered again and started trickling down her cheeks. Jack had been wonderful last weekend, though he hadn't liked her having to use the breast pump. She had seen the recoil in his eyes, the frown, the silent wish it wasn't happening. She had given the excuse of a heavy workload to put him off coming to her flat the past two nights, not wanting him to see her discomfort.

He would undoubtedly blame Charlotte, and everything would start going wrong. Maybe it was cowardice on her part, avoiding problems that might put him off the fatherhood scene. Testing his resolve didn't seem like a good idea any more. Making love had probably been a big mistake. She wanted him too much.

"Give me Jack's number," Sally commanded.

"What for?"

"You can't manage this alone, Nina."

"Other single mothers must," she argued.

"What's the point in hiding it? Jack's either there for you or he isn't. Better find that out now, Nina."

Relentless logic.

The fear of losing him persisted. "It's only about eleven o'clock. He'll be busy at work, and it mightn't turn out to be as bad as you think, Sally."

Her desperate optimism earned a derisive snort. "Your temperature's sky-high. If Jack won't take over with Charlotte when you're sick, he's not worth having," Sally declared, her vision unclouded by emotional bias. "She may have to be bottle-fed. And that means shopping for all the necessary stuff. Now is the time for all good men to come to the aid of the party. Give me his number."

Nina's head whirled. Too much to do, and she was too weak and woozy to do it. Besides, Sally was only speaking the inescapable truth. If Jack couldn't handle this, it boded ill for a future together. She gave his number, and Sally simultaneously pressed it into the car phone.

"Jack. It's Sally. Don't talk. Listen. We haven't got time for unnecessary chat. I'm almost at the doctor's surgery with Nina, and she's in trouble. Running a fever and pain in her breasts. She might have to go into hospital."

"Hospital!" Nina groaned, the future getting blacker by the minute.

Sally ignored her. "Are you okay to help with the baby?"

"Tell me what to do and I'll do it," came the quick, decisive reply.

"Go to a chemist shop and buy up whatever you'll need to feed a newborn baby. Tins of formula, bottles, teats, sterilising solution. Ask the pharamacist. He should know everything. It might not be necessary, but it's better to be prepared. You can always exchange these items for other stuff. Next feed is two o'clock, but Charlotte might want it before then."

"I'll go right now."

"Hold it! If Nina has to go to hospital, can you step in and take over with Charlotte?"

"No problem. I'll take her home with me. Nina, too, if the doctor only gives her medication. I'll look after both of them."

"Sure you can handle it?"

"They're my family. Thanks for letting me know, Sally."

"I left my secretary with the baby at the flat. I'll report to her when I know more."

"I'll go to the flat as soon as I have the stuff for Charlotte."

"Right. Bye for now."

Charlotte. He'd called her Charlotte. Surely that had to be a good sign, Nina told herself. And the possessive way he'd said *my family* ... Jack had the best of intentions. She didn't know why she was crying. The tears rolled from a seemingly unstoppable well.

"That guy is coming through really well, Nina," Sally asserted as she drove her BMW into the parking lot behind the medical centre. "His heart is in the right place. Having met countless bridegrooms in my time as a wedding director, let me tell you Jack scores a high distinction in many areas."

"Thanks, Sally." Nina managed to choke the words out. She wished she'd consulted Sally before she'd reached this awful state.

"Now let's get you inside to the doctor."

It was out of her hands now, Nina thought. Fate had done it to her again, throwing her a curve she could never have anticipated. She couldn't exercise any control over where it would end. It was all up to Jack to make it come out right.

If he had the heart for it.

CHAPTER SIXTEEN

CHARLIE girl was yelling her lungs out and wouldn't listen to a word Jack said. He walked her up and down Nina's living room, rubbing and patting her back with no better result. The kid was beyond reason and comfort. Jack was desperate for news of Nina and more instructions when the telephone rang.

"I'll answer that," he shouted at Sally's secretary, and quickly thrust the baby into her arms. "Take her into the bedroom and shut the door. I don't want Nina hearing her over the phone and getting upset. Hurry!"

He grabbed the receiver the moment the door shut. "It's Jack. How's Nina?" he demanded anxiously.

"Worst-case scenario. Abscesses. The doctor's given her intravenous antibiotics and booked her in at Royal North Shore Hospital. I'm taking her there now. A surgeon will see her this afternoon."

"A surgeon?" Alarm shot through him.

"No big deal. It's called incision and drainage. Nina will have a general anaesthetic."

"That could make her pretty damned sick," he said worriedly, his gut twisting at what she had to go through.

"She is pretty damned sick. They'll probably hold her in hospital for a couple of days. Have you got everything for Charlotte?"

It hit him with nerve-shattering force that he was on his own with the kid. Not for an hour or two. For a couple of days! And nights! No fall-back situation with Nina on hand. The responsibility was all his. He fought down an incipient sense of panic. Hadn't he said all along that a little kid couldn't beat him?

"All equipped and ready to go," he said, firmly projecting confidence. "Tell Nina not to worry. Tell her Charlotte couldn't have a more competent dad. I'll handle everything at this end."

Charlotte... That's what Nina called her. Since he had to be both Mum and Dad to the kid, he'd better use that name, too. Give himself double-barrelled power.

"Good," Sally said approvingly, as though she'd heard his thought. "I'll come over to your place this evening and mind Charlotte while you visit Nina and reassure her. Okay?"

Relief flooded through him. He wasn't really on his own. Sally would help if needed. And there were Maurice and Ingrid and any number of friends he could call on. The panic receded somewhat.

"That would be great, Sally. Give Nina my love. And thanks again," he said with sincere gratitude for her forethought and friendship.

Jack put the receiver down and took several deep breaths to unwind the knots in his stomach

and get some oxygen into his brain. He was going
to need a clear head and a cast-iron constitution.
The kid's life and well-being were in his hands.

It suddenly struck him that depending on
friends to deal with this baby emergency could
be viewed by Nina as a cop-out. In actual fact it
was a cop-out.

Charlotte was his kid. He'd told Nina no
nannies. He was not going to shunt his kid off
onto anyone else. This was the big one. The
proving ground. He had to make a success of it,
or Nina would wipe him off and shut him out
forever. Rightly so. If he couldn't be a responsible father in a crisis, he didn't deserve any
further consideration.

With steely resolution he marched down the
hall and into the bedroom. Charlotte was still
bawling. He took her from Sally's secretary and
perched her against his shoulder so her ear was
fairly close to his mouth. He pitched his voice
low and intense and projected urgent command.

"Listen up, kid."

The bawling hiccupped to a halt. Jack patted
her back in warm approval as he spelled out the
problem.

"You and I need to come to an accommodation. Just remember, we're in this together. You
and me, kid. We did the damage, and now your
mum's out of action. What's more, we've got to
come through this with top marks."

A loud burp exploded near his neck.

"That's good," Jack encouraged. "Don't start crying again. It'll only give you more wind. Going onto a bottle after being on your mum's breast may not be—"

A full-blooded scream told Jack in no uncertain terms this communication was not welcome. It raised the hair on the back of his neck. Sheer terror was electrifying. He did his best to rectify his mistake and failed miserably.

Patting didn't soothe Charlotte. Rocking didn't help. She paid absolutely no attention to his claim that everything would be all right if she just trusted him. The little legs kicked, tiny fists were clenched and waving aggressively, face screwed up in constant yelling mode, body contorting against every attempt to comfort. Jack had joked with his friends about babies from hell. His heart quailed.

With another burst of determination, he forced his mind clear of the paralysing noise. There was only one answer to this. His friends had informed him that car motion acted like a sleeping pill for babies. He had to load Charlotte into the Rover and hit the road. If she didn't calm down, he had no hope of feeding her from a bottle.

Getting the formula right for her loomed ahead of him. He couldn't expect to strike it lucky the first time around. The pharmacist had suggested he take three different tins of it, in case one or the other didn't suit her taste. He had to try out different teats, as well. Bottle-feeding was a complicated business. He needed Charlotte's full cooperation if they were to find an agreeable solution.

He lowered the wildly fractious kid into the capsule and used the bunny rug like a straitjacket to hold her tucked in. Charlotte did her fighting best to wreck his arrangement. Fortunately, he had everything ready to go. Sally's secretary had been most helpful, packing for Nina while he had loaded all the baby stuff into the Rover.

With Nina ill, he wanted the quickest and smoothest transfer to his home. It gave him a sick, hollow feeling to think of her going to hospital instead of coming home with him. Making it worse was the frantic fear of failing the fatherhood test.

He passed on Sally's report to her secretary as she accompanied him out to the street and watched him anchor the capsule to the back seat.

"Good luck!" she said with feeling.

He waved a salute and climbed into the driver's seat, thinking he needed all the luck he could get in these circumstances but admitting such a need sounded weak. This was a time for unshakable strength. He had to show Nina he was a rock she could always lean on. Charlotte, too.

He did his best to ignore the wailing from the back seat as he started the engine and headed for home. It took Charlotte the length of Mowbray Road to the Pacific Highway to quiet down. Jack blessed the friends who'd told him about the car-motion trick.

With peace momentarily reigning, Jack moved his brain into high gear and activated the car phone to set the next critical step in motion. He'd told his two apprentices he'd be bringing his family home and they were to be on standby to help.

Gary, his older apprentice, answered the call. "I'll be at Boundary Street in a few minutes," Jack informed him briskly. "Nina's gone to hospital so I'm on my own with the kid. I need all the baby stuff out of the Rover and inside as fast as possible, so come running when I pull up."

"We'll be ready for you, Jack. Anything else?"

Jack thought swiftly. "Yes. Find the biggest pots in the kitchen, fill them with hot water and put them on the stove to boil. Quickest way to sterilise bottles and teats."

"Right."

"That's it for now."

It wasn't a cop-out to use his apprentices, Jack reasoned. He was still the one in charge, and there was no telling how quickly Charlotte would wake up and demand to be fed. It was best to be ready to give satisfaction. If he could. Pleased with his forethought, Jack concentrated on picking the fastest lane through the traffic.

Gary and Ben were only in their late teens, but he'd found them completely reliable, and meticulous in following his instructions. They had the same innate drive to get things right as he had, an important character trait for French polishing. Anyone who worked with him had to take pride in doing and finishing a job properly, down to the finest detail.

Jack reflected it was lucky all his pots were stainless steel. No possible mistake with them. The pharmacist had warned him against aluminium pots for use in sterilising. Of course, once he was over the hump of the first couple of feeds, he'd use the sterilising solution and equipment he'd bought, but that took six hours. Deal with the emergency first, Jack reasoned, then establish a routine. He had to keep thinking positively.

Operation Arrival went as efficiently as Jack could hope for. "We'll set up in the breakfast room," he instructed, and the boys were right on his heels with the first load of baby necessities— the bath, the change table, the nursery bucket, the shopping. Spike fell into step on the other side of the capsule, keeping an eye on the new pup as Jack carried it inside.

The breakfast room was open to the kitchen. The boys usually ate their lunch there. It had a good solid oak table with half a dozen sturdy chairs around it. A TV set and one comfortable recliner chair for Jack's convenience comprised the rest of the furniture. There was plenty of space to set up the change table and all the paraphernalia that went with it. A bathroom was just off the kitchen, so the major work areas for a baby crisis were handy.

Jack put the capsule down near the TV set, out of the way of the action. "Watch her, Spike. Anything wrong, let me know."

The dog squatted, sticking his head over the side of the capsule for a closer look. It was a pity the pup was all covered up. It smelled as though it needed a good lick.

Jack unpacked the shopping, loading it along the kitchen counter for easy access. The boys brought in the bags of nappies, Nina's suitcase and the load of clothes and other stuff he'd packed for Charlotte.

"That's everything, Jack," Ben assured him. He was seventeen, a cheery-faced, red-haired kid who was always eager to please.

"Great. You guys start sterilising the bottles and teats while I get the change table ready for action."

"Why are we boiling up nine bottles?" Gary asked. He was a thin, wiry, intense nineteen-year-old who had a passion for knowing the whys and wherefores. As a statement of rebellion against standard conformity he tied his long brown hair in a ponytail and wore one earring. "I didn't think a baby could drink that much," he added with a frown.

"Mathematics, Gary. We've got three different formulas to try and three different teats, a fast flow, medium flow and slow flow. I want every combination ready, three bottles of each formula with each size teat on them. That way we can find out what suits the kid best without too much delay in between trial and error.''

''If we boil the teats in three different pots we won't get the sizes mixed up,'' Ben suggested.

''Good idea,'' Jack said, warmly approving. Nothing like effective and efficient initiatives to get a project off the ground. ''You're in charge of that, Ben. Only five minutes for the teats. Ten minutes for the bottles. I'd better get some towels out of the linen cupboard. This kid can be a champion spewer if we get it wrong for her.''

Jack privately congratulated himself on sounding calm and practical and in control. He collected a box of tissues and some face washers, as well. Being prepared for the worst would stop any panic setting in. He had to keep hoping the worst wasn't beyond his capabilities. He double-checked that he had every possible need assembled on the change table, then joined the boys in the kitchen.

Charlotte—bless her little heart—slept on as Jack and his two helpers started mixing the formulas. The assembly line of bottles was quickly achieved. Each set of three was placed in a pot of lukewarm water so the formula would come out at the right temperature.

Jack congratulated his boys on having done a great job. The initial pressure was off, and they were all feeling pleased with themselves when a mewling cry signalled time up. Spike leapt up and barked a warning. Action stations again.

Jack quelled a twinge of fear that all the preparation in the world might be of no avail if Charlotte felt they'd lost the plot her life had followed since she was born. Dogs sensed fear. For all he knew, babies did, too. *I'm a rock*, he sternly told himself, and rapped out an order to demonstrate his unshakability.

"Test the temperature of the formula while I change her nappy."

"How do we do that?" Gary asked.

"Sprinkle some on your wrist. Shouldn't be any hotter or colder than your skin."

He scooped Charlotte out of the capsule just as she was screwing up her face for a full-blooded yell. The shock of being lifted opened her eyes and turned the yell into a splutter.

"It's okay. Your dad's going to take care of business," he assured her as he carried her to the change table.

She kept her eyes on him as he disposed of her wet nappy. Spike almost upset everything, standing on his hind legs and resting his forepaws on the table so he could get a proper view of proceedings. His weight pushed the lightweight table, rocking it for a moment, but he quickly adjusted his balance.

"Gently does it, Spike," Jack admonished him, desperately controlling a wild flutter of apprehension. He didn't want Charlotte's confidence in him undermined before he'd even started to offer her a bottle.

Luckily Spike provided distraction, Charlotte transferring her wide-eyed and wary gaze to the dog. Spike sniffed the baby oil. He sniffed the talcum powder. He sniffed the fresh nappy Jack fastened around the pup. It was all very curious.

"There you go," Jack said triumphantly, putting her legs into the body suit. "Your mum couldn't do it any better."

Big round eyes looked up at him. Jack sensed a belligerent challenge, possibly even a clash of wills in the offing. All was not right in her world. She knew it, and she was not about to be fooled.

"This next bit is going to be strange to you, Charlotte," he warned respectfully as he did up the press studs. "Nothing can really take the place of your mum, but there are some things you've got to accept in life, like it or not. It's up to you to make your choice of the options I've lined up. And Charlotte—" his voice gathered in eloquent appeal "—please try to understand this is all there is for you."

The grave look she returned was full of suspicion. Jack was full of trepidation. But he'd told her the truth, and what more could he do? Life did bowl a curve sometimes. One had to adjust and move on. He hadn't planned on being a father, and here he was, taking on the role of both parents.

"Going to do a good job of it, too," he muttered as he carried Charlotte over to the breakfast table and sat down, cradling her in the crook of his arm. He tucked a hand towel under her chin to catch spillage and spread a bath towel over his knees for bigger accidents.

"Temperature's fine, Jack," Gary declared.

"Formula one, slow-flow teat," Jack instructed.

Ben handed him the bottle. The boys stood by to watch the baby's response. Having sniffed the nappy that had been dropped into the nursery bucket, Spike lined up with them. All eyes were on the teat going into Charlotte's mouth.

"She's sucking," Ben said excitedly.

"Yeah, but is she getting any?" Gary questioned.

The little jaws worked away for a minute or so and gave up. She spat the teat, screwed up her face and bawled her frustration.

Jack's stomach started tying itself in knots again. He checked the level of formula in the bottle. Hardly any gone. "Medium flow," he commanded, willing himself to stay on top of the crisis despite his misgivings about Charlotte's willingness to adapt to adverse circumstances.

Ben took the discard bottle. Gary handed him the next tryout. Spike whined at the strange pup. She stopped her weird barking and looked at him. Jack shoved the new teat into her mouth, and Charlotte latched onto it. She sucked. Not for long. Her mouth turned down, and the formula dribbled out the corners of it. "Yuk!" was written all over her face.

"I can tell you, kid," Jack said sharply. "None of it's going to taste exactly like mother's milk."

He heard himself cracking and appreciated, for the first time, how a baby could reduce even the most reasonable adult to a quivering wreck. He pulled himself back from the brink and got on with the job, handing the bad-taste bottle to Gary. "Formula one's a reject. Let's try formula two, medium flow."

Jack wiped away all trace of the yukky dribble before offering the next bottle. He didn't want Charlotte to get confused, thinking it was the same taste. She needed food. One way or another, he had to get it right for her.

She attacked the new teat like a threshing machine. For the next five minutes it looked as though formula two was a winner. Then her stomach staged a revolt. The formula came back out like a gusher. The towels took a beating. Gary removed them to the laundry. Ben brought some more. Jack did his best to soothe Charlotte, holding her up to his shoulder and patting comfort. She vomited down his back.

Nightmare alley, Jack thought, struggling to keep his anxiety under control. Spike examined the mess and decided not to lick it up. Gary manfully took on the cleaning duty. Jack juggled Charlotte as Ben helped him strip off his soiled shirt.

Having emptied her stomach, Charlotte yelled for more food. "Formula three, medium flow," Jack called, an edge of desperation creeping into his voice. He settled her on his arm again and addressed her on the seriousness of the situation.

"This is the last stop, Charlotte. You've run out of choices. Think about it."

"Maybe we should try slow flow again, Jack," Ben suggested anxiously. "Let her get used to the taste before it hits her tummy."

Jack nodded, his mind almost numb with the possibility of all-out disaster. "Good thinking. Go slow might do the trick."

Ben quickly swapped the bottles, and they all held their breaths as Charlotte started working the teat, more cautiously this time. She had a brooding look on her face. Her eyes clung to Jack's. "This is the good stuff," he crooned. At this point, propaganda was his last resort.

Her face slowly cleared of the suspicion they were poisoning her. Her sucking settled into a steady rhythm, and the content in the bottle gradually lowered.

"We've got it," Ben crowed.

"That's the one, all right," Gary happily agreed.

Jack's nerves sang a song of relief. To keep the sense of a positive roll moving forward, he directed the logical conclusion to this critical exercise.

"Okay, guys. We throw out the first two formulas and put the slow teats on the other two bottles of this lot. Store them in the fridge for later."

He hoped Charlotte was storing this formula in her memory cells and would recognise it as the good stuff at future feeds. Scientific process was

fine in theory, but human beings were both con-
trary and unpredictable. Jack had been shaken
into an acute realisation that he was holding a
miniature human being with a mind and stomach
of its own, who was totally dependent on his
meeting its needs. It was a highly sobering and
humbling experience.

"Do we use the sterilising solution for the spare
bottles now, Jack?" Gary checked.

"Yes. Wash them up and dob them in."

High on success, the boys went back to kitchen
duty. Spike remained on watch, his canine mind
intent on collecting a bank of information on this
new species of pup. Jack gradually relaxed, happy
that Charlotte had apparently accepted the inevitable, at least for the time being. Maybe the
surrender was due to exhaustion or hopeless resignation, but Jack preferred to look on the
brighter side. His kid was not about to die of
thirst or starvation. Thus far she was safe with
him. As he'd promised her she would be.

"Your mum would be proud of you,
Charlotte," he told her. "This is a big step to
take for a little kid, and you're doing great."

The teat dropped out as she hiccupped.

Was this another protest on the way? "Got
some wind?" Jack asked hopefully.

He put the bottle on the table so he could give
her back a gentle rub. Two big burps. No sicking
up. He grinned at the boys, who had stopped
work to watch the outcome. "No worries," he

assured them, almost dizzy with relief as he settled Charlotte onto his other arm.

"See? Your dad can change sides just like your mum. Here comes the good stuff." He didn't care if he looked or sounded fatuous. He zoomed the bottle down to her mouth, and she latched on again. He felt a rush of paternal pride. "You're a champion kid, Charlotte. A real fast learner."

Spike barked agreement and trotted around the chair to take up watch on the other side. The hump of the current crisis was definitely over.

"Thanks for the teamwork, guys," Jack said warmly. "It could have been rough without your first-rate assistance."

Gary grinned. "New experience to chalk up."

"Yeah," Ben agreed, matching his work-mate's grin. "Operation Bottle-feed. That's a good one, isn't it, Gary?"

They laughed, happy to have been of help.

Jack smiled at Charlotte. They had all learned something today. It brought a new sense of closeness, a bonding that was different from anything Jack had felt before. This little-bitty human being was precious to him. He wanted her to be happy. With him. With the world. With everything. Whatever it took, he'd manage it somehow.

Spike shuffled forward and laid his head on Jack's lap, claiming his place in the family, too. Jack ruffled the long, shaggy hair. If only Nina were here with them. A wave of misery flattened any sense of euphoria at having come through the crucible of full, hands-on fatherhood.

Nina must be going through hell. He hoped the medical staff at the hospital were giving her adequate pain-killers as well as antibiotics. He'd raise a ruckus tonight if they weren't.

He hadn't seen her for almost three days. Her choice, not his. The suspicion rose that she hadn't felt well and had hidden it from him, though why she would keep it to herself was beyond his comprehension. Didn't she realise he would do anything for her?

Something was wrong with Nina's thinking. She had called for Sally's help, not his. Tonight he would have to find out why she hadn't turned to him. She should have done, instinctively, automatically. Did she still not trust him to do right by Charlotte?

Jack shook his head in bewilderment. His gaze fell on the baby. She'd stopped sucking. Her mouth was slack, her eyes closed, and her sweet little face glowed with replete contentment. It gave his heart a real boost, filling it with so many good feelings his underlying anxieties were momentarily forgotten. *My kid*, he thought. *Mine and Nina's.*

At least he could lift one worry off Nina's mind.

Operation Bottle-feed successful.

CHAPTER SEVENTEEN

"NINA?"

Jack's voice, soft and strained with concern. Sluggishly she opened her eyes. The curtain was drawn around her bed. She'd been sleeping since the surgeon's visit. He'd examined her and explained what he was going to do in the morning. The pain tablets were good. If she kept still, the discomfort could be held at a distance. But she needed to see Jack, talk to him. She slowly turned her head.

"Don't move if it hurts," he said anxiously, springing up from the chair to lean over her.

"Charlotte?" It came out like a croak. Her throat was dry.

"She's fine. Sally's with her while I'm here. She's taken to the bottle okay, Nina. I've fed her two lots of formula. She's not fretting or playing up. Everything's going well. When I left she was fast asleep. No problem."

Nina knew she should feel relieved, pleased that Jack was coping with their baby. It was ridiculous to feel so bereft and useless. Tears welled into her eyes, great globs of self-pity. It wasn't fair this had happened to her. All the hard months of her pregnancy, fiercely resolving to be everything to her child, and she couldn't even feed her baby. She shut her eyes to stop the tears from overflowing, but they squeezed through her lashes.

Jack's hand gently brushed her hair from her forehead. "Is it terribly painful, Nina? Do you want me to fetch a nurse?"

"No."

"Then what's wrong, love?"

The deep caring in his voice twisted her heart. "I'm a failure," she blurted out.

"No, you're not," he strongly asserted. "Sally told me your designs for Belinda Pinkerton's wedding are brilliant. You've got great talent, Nina, and once people start seeing it..."

She moved her head fretfully. "I'm a failure as a mother. I let you get in the way, Jack."

His hand stilled, then withdrew. She heard the chair being drawn closer, the squeak of its cushion as he sat down. The sense of apartness made her feel worse, as though she was losing everything.

"How, Nina?" he asked quietly.

She had to swallow hard to get rid of the lump in her throat. She opened her eyes and looked at him with aching regret. "I didn't want you to know I had a problem. I hoped it would get better. I wanted it to go away. If it wasn't for you and my delaying getting help..." Tears swam again. "I'd still be feeding Charlotte."

"Why didn't you want me to know?" He shook his head in hurt confusion. "Love is about sharing. Both the good and the bad."

"I didn't want the bad to rebound on Charlotte. You blaming her and resenting her."

"I don't!" he cried, standing in agitation, his hands slicing the air in frustration as he pulled himself back from pressing his case with more physical persuasion. "I wouldn't, Nina!" he pleaded. "She's not to blame for anything. She's just an innocent little kid, for God's sake!"

His vehemence made her head pound. Her mind clutched wearily at the truth he spoke and limply let it go. Reason and logic could be argued until the end of time. It made no difference to the realities seeded by emotions.

"You hated seeing me use the breast pump," she said flatly.

It silenced him, cut the feet out from under his principled posture. Principles were fine things. The problem was in living up to them. He sank back onto the chair. He expelled a long breath as though trying to lower a dangerous high of pent-up feelings. His face was grim, jawline tight, eyes shuttered as he leaned forward, resting his elbows on his knees.

"That's true. I did," he admitted, as though tearing the words from his conscience. "Though not for the reasons you attribute to me, Nina. It was because *I* felt guilty."

She frowned, not understanding.

With an anguished look at her, he reached out and stroked his fingers gently over the hand lying close to him. "Please listen to me, Nina. I'm sorry you read different things into my feelings. The last thing I wanted was to give you pain.''

Her fingers lifted instinctively to tangle with his, to link, wanting his warmth, wanting so much more from him. Her eyes clung to his in hope, aching for him to allay the apartness she felt.

''The first night we made love, I had a talk to Charlotte beforehand, telling her it would be good if she slept through,'' he confessed. ''She did. With the result that you had to use a breast pump, which you obviously found unpleasant. I then told Charlotte she'd better wake up as usual, but she'd got the hang of sleeping through and there was nothing I could do about it. You shouldn't give a little kid confused messages, on again, off again. It wasn't her fault.''

Nina stared incredulously at him. He really thought Charlotte took in what he said to her?

''None of this is her fault.'' His eyes begged her forgiveness. ''It was me. It was me!'' His face twisted with guilt. ''I was being selfish, wanting us to have the night together like we used to. I'm dreadfully sorry, Nina. I just didn't realise how it would affect you.''

Nina's stomach clenched. She had misunderstood, misjudged. It was crazy for Jack to have felt guilty, but she could see that he did, given his propensity for fantasy communication with his dog and Charlotte.

''If you'd shared your worries with me, I could have helped,'' he went on regretfully. ''Told you about cabbage leaves. It might have saved you all this pain.''

''Cabbage leaves?'' she repeated dazedly.

''One of my friends told me about them. His wife got sore breasts from feeding their baby, and she used a cabbage leaf compress in her bra to get them better. It worked, too.''

''Why? How?'' Nina couldn't believe it.

Jack shrugged. ''There's no known scientific reason for it, but it does work. You keep the cabbage in the refrigerator so the leaves form a cold compress. When they warm up in the bra you replace them with cold ones again. My friend was joking about how many cabbages he had in his fridge, but he wasn't joking about it fixing up the problem. We could have tried it, Nina.''

We... It was she who had set them apart, not Jack. She should have given him the benefit of the doubt and put fear aside.

''I know lots of things about problems with babies,'' he added anxiously. ''My friends have poured them out to me. I guess that's why I thought they were little monsters. Nobody bothered telling me the best things. Like the funny expressions Charlotte gets on her face and how good it feels when she's happy.''

Her heart swelled with so many mixed emotions Nina couldn't find words for them. The realisation thumped into her mind that it was her fault it had come to this, her fault for not opening up to Jack, not trusting him, her fault she could no longer feed her baby. It would have been all right if only she had spoken, shared, as Jack said they should, the bad, as well as the good. How had she got so twisted up?

Her eyes filled with more tears.

"Don't cry, love," Jack begged. "Tell me what I can do." He grabbed some tissues and gently dabbed the wet streams trickling down her cheeks. "If there's something you want..."

"I'm sorry," she choked out. He wasn't to blame at all. She was.

"It's okay. If it helps to cry, you cry. But don't think you're a failure as a mother, Nina," he said earnestly. "You're a wonderful mother. The best. Any kid would be lucky to have you as their mum. The breastfeeding bit doesn't matter. It's the love that counts, and Charlotte knows she's loved."

The warmth in his voice washed over her, soothing the painful torments in her mind. He dabbed her cheeks again as she struggled for control of her tear ducts. Her head ached, her body ached and her heart ached. She was a mess. Nevertheless, she pushed herself to make the effort to speak.

"Thanks for coming to the rescue, Jack. With Charlotte, I mean."

"I'm her dad," he said gruffly. "I wish you'd take that on board, Nina. You're not alone. Unless you really prefer it that way."

His pained expression needed answering. "I don't," she said simply.

His eyes scanned hers, searing them with his doubts as to her underlying wishes and feelings. "It doesn't add up, Nina," he said softly. "You say you love me. You say you're giving me a chance. Yet you turned to Sally, not to me. It was Sally who called me to the rescue. You shut me out. Again."

It was not a bitter accusation, more a restrained statement of fact, all the more powerful in tearing at the reservations she had held about him.

He took a deep breath, and there was a flicker of compassion in his eyes as he went on. "I appreciate where you're coming from, Nina, but I have scars, too. We all carry baggage of one description or another. In many ways my parents shut me out of their lives. I wasn't abused. I was simply and effectively sidelined. Ignored for the most part."

His tone was matter-of-fact, not begging pity or even sympathy, but the loneliness of a long-distance runner was behind the words.

"I understand why you shut me out of your pregnancy, though your decision took no account of my love for you," he went on. "It painted me as not worth consideration. Like today. How do you think it makes me feel, Nina, to know you chose not to call on me? To keep it all to yourself?"

She hadn't seen it that way. She hadn't wanted to bother him . . . a different form of consideration. "You were very much on my mind, Jack," she pleaded.

He shook his head. "Negatively, not positively. I want to be involved, not set aside. And for you to risk this kind of suffering rather than open your door to me, it makes me wonder if I'm doing wrong in thrusting myself into your life again."

"No. I do want you, Jack," she cried. "I want you so much, I'm frightened of anything that might drive you away."

"Only you can drive me away." His voice throbbed with raw intensity. "I keep knocking on your door. You open it. You shut it. Putting me outside doesn't make me feel wanted, Nina. I don't even do that to my dog."

She cringed at the blunt indictment of the way she had treated him. She had no excuse. She had seen everything from her own prejudicial point of view. Tunnel vision. With growing horror she realised she had done to Jack what her parents had done to her—rejected him, lowered his sense of self-worth, focused on her own feelings without considering the effect on him. Just because he was a man didn't mean he was immune to the same hurts she had known.

He grimaced. "I probably shouldn't have brought this up when you're so ill. Not the time nor the place."

"Yes, it is, Jack," she whispered, squeezing his hand. "You needed to say it, and I needed to hear it."

He gave her a crooked half-smile. "As long as you're reassured that Charlotte is safe with me."

"I am. Thank you. For many things."

It wasn't enough, not the touch or the words. She sensed his inner tension, the restraint he was constructing, sealing off the wounds of mistrust and moving silently but resolutely to that place of self-sufficiency he had learned to exist in long before they had ever met. No doubt he had returned there during the estranged months of her pregnancy. It was Jack's survival ground, come what may.

"I brought in your toiletries and a set of fresh clothes for when you leave," he said flatly.

Easier to deal with the superficial mechanics of life than the hidden areas, Nina thought. Jack withdrew his hand and bent to unpack an overnight bag. The physical separation made her even more tensely aware of the effect her reluctance to involve him was having, the loss of true intimacy, the protective shield she had raised, driving Jack to start raising his own.

Having stowed her belongings in the drawers of the bedside cabinet, he resumed his seat, facing her with a bleak and determined expression. It alarmed Nina. He had come here caring about her, and she had blamed him for her own failure. The cost of that mistake was building up.

"Sally told me you'll be raw and sore for a week or so. I've planned for both you and Charlotte to stay with me. If it's not what you want, Nina . . . If you'd rather return to your flat and arrange other help—''

"No." She had to stop his retreat from her. "If it's not too much trouble for you . . ." That sounded weak and uncertain. "I mean—"

"Don't feel obliged to come to me just because I took responsibility for Charlotte while you're in here," he added before she could find a more positive reply. "If I've assumed too much, bulldozing you into a situation that's distressing you, it's better we settle it now. It was never my intention to hurt you. Say the word and I'll take everything back to your flat."

"No. I want to come to you," she said with as much strength as she could muster.

His direct gaze left no room for prevarication. "As a halfway house or a serious commitment, Nina? Please be honest with me."

Her heart started galloping. How could she promise the level of absolute trust he wanted when she couldn't trust herself to deliver on it? If it were possible to throw a switch that would alter or adjust all the negative circuits in her brain, she would. It wasn't her intention to hurt, either.

"Will you give me another chance, Jack?" she pleaded. "I'll do my best to sort myself out."

"It doesn't have to be done by yourself, Nina. My door is open to you, and I'm always ready to listen." Frustration threaded his voice. "If you'll only be honest with me."

"Yes. I realise that now," she said earnestly.

His face slowly relaxed into a half-smile of wry appeal. "Charlotte is not just yours, Nina. She's part of both of us. It's not two against one. It's the three of us."

"Yes," she agreed, seizing the concept with desperate energy. "Do you love her, Jack?"

He looked blank, as though he'd lost connection with her train of thought.

"Charlotte, our baby. Do you love her?" she repeated anxiously, needing to hear him say it.

The light switched on behind his eyes again. He reached out and took her hand, pressing it with convincing fervour as he answered, "Yes. Yes, I do." He sounded almost surprised at his own words.

Was it true?

"We're a family," he added insistently.

Nina clutched at that concept, too, eager to push aside the single-parent status she had carried for so long. She didn't have to be a single parent. She didn't want to be. Jack was giving her a chance to have it all... the three of them.

"A family," she repeated, fiercely resolving to embrace the idea in every way. No shut doors. The sense of togetherness had to be held and nurtured. Belonging to each other—that was what family should mean. Belonging so deeply that love and trust and support could be taken for granted.

Her inner turmoil eased. It slid into her mind that Jack was right in saying human beings made life more complex than it had to be. Of course, he must love Charlotte. He wouldn't be asking for honesty if he wasn't prepared to give it himself. She laced her fingers through his and closed her eyes, concentrating on the warmth and strength of his touch.

Together...

A family.

CHAPTER EIGHTEEN

FEELING raw and sore for a week was no exaggeration, Nina discovered. She could not have coped alone, even if she had wanted to. Going home with Jack proved to be the best solution to everything. It was a revelation in so many reassuring ways. Nina was constantly being shamed for having harboured any doubts and fears about a future with him.

He was kindness itself in looking after her and seeing to her needs. The community nurse visited every day to supervise her medication and recovery. Jack fed her, washed her, helped her do whatever she wanted and gave her loving company.

If she was awake he shared Charlotte's feeding times with her. It was too painful for her to hold the baby, but she was happy to watch Jack handling their child, talking away as though Charlotte understood him perfectly and always including Nina in the conversation, welding them into a family unit. He'd put a rocking chair in the bedroom, and he'd sit for hours sometimes, beaming with love and pleasure in both of them.

When she had first seen Charlotte taking eagerly to the bottle, Nina had felt a deeply distressing confusion. Had she only imagined the special bonding between mother and child arising from the physical connection of breastfeeding? It hurt to feel she wasn't necessary at all. Not even missed. Left fragile in every sense by the operation, she had been unable to block a rush of tears.

"It's no different to her," she blurted out in answer to Jack's concern. "The bottle is just as good."

"It might be now she's got used to it, Nina, but let me tell you she gave us the rounds of the kitchen the first time up," Jack said with an expressive roll of his eyes. "All of us were on tenterhooks, trying to please her with a substitute, and she knew jolly well she wasn't getting mother's milk."

It distracted Nina from her sense of loss. "All of you? Who do you mean?"

"Gary and Ben and Spike. I talked Charlotte through it while they gave me backup support."

Nina listened in amazement as he described his scientific method of trial and error, the assistance given by his apprentices, Charlotte's reactions, the advice he had given her and the final acceptance of the third formula. She wished it had all been taped on video film, the three men handing bottles around, the dog getting in on the act, the baby the focus of all attention and efforts to please, missing her mother in no uncertain terms.

"You did wonderfully well, Jack," Nina said in sincere admiration, immeasurably cheered by this story.

His smile gave her heart another lift. Everyone wanted approval, she thought. And praise. Recognition of what was given. Love and appreciation went hand in hand.

"Try not to be upset about the bottle-feeding, Nina," he urged, his green eyes soft with warm sympathy. "I know it's a disappointment to you, but next time we'll know better. You'll be able to breastfeed as long as you want to."

"Next time?" she echoed uncertainly.

"Uh..." He looked discomfited and tried to dismiss it. "Just an idea I had. Bit premature. Forget it. The important thing is Charlotte's okay. Nothing for you to worry about."

"You're not being honest with me, Jack," she chided. "Why not play the idea past me?"

He shrugged and grimaced appealingly. "It sounds like I'm assuming too much. You said not to rush you. Let it go for now, Nina."

"I've adopted an open-door policy. I'm listening, Jack," she said persuasively, wanting to know his innermost thoughts and dreams.

He gave her the direct look that zinged straight into her heart. He hesitated for a few moments, needing to reassure himself he wasn't about to make a mistake. She returned his gaze steadily, projecting her desire to share in every sense.

"I didn't like being an only kid, Nina," he said tentatively. "Since we've got Charlotte...I

thought, maybe in a year or two...if you felt up
to it..."

"We add to the family?"

"What do you think?" he asked warily. "If
you'd prefer to leave it at one... It was just an
idea. It's been growing on me this past week. I
mean, I can't imagine life without Charlotte now.
I really love this kid. If we had more, there'd be
plenty of love around for everyone, wouldn't
there?"

Nina had a mad desire to laugh. She had been
so hopelessly and wildly wrong about Jack, it was
almost funny. But it wasn't, really. It had very
nearly been tragic. Again tears threatened. She
struggled for control, then smiled to set him at
ease.

"I was an only child, too. I know what you
mean, Jack. It would be good for Charlotte to
have a brother or sister."

His face broke into a pleased grin. "Hear that,
kid?" he asked Charlotte, who promptly stopped
guzzling to give him her full attention. "You
might rule the roost, but you're going to have
company."

She blew him a raspberry.

"There you go, getting impertinent again. I'll
tell Spike on you if you don't show proper
respect."

The dog, who had squatted beside the rocking
chair, leapt up to check what was going on. He
looked at Charlotte. Charlotte looked him
straight in the eye, as though imparting the

message that he needn't think he could be inter-
fering between her and her father, then lifted her
gaze to Jack and opened her mouth for the teat
again.

It was enough to make Nina start wondering
if there was more to instinctive communication
than she had credited.

Over the next few days, it became very evident
that Jack had an innate talent for family. He
called his apprentices "his boys", giving them a
strong sense of being on the team, and they
looked up to him as though he was a second
father to them. Spike dogged his footsteps everywhere and was naturally included in practically
every activity. Charlotte, "the kid" or, Nina suspected, "the pup" in Spike's mind—was adopted
by all of them.

Eventually the community nurse declared Nina
healed. Having accompanied her to the front
door, thanking her for the help and advice given,
Nina went in search of Jack and Charlotte to give
them the good news. She heard voices coming
from the rumpus room, where Jack did his final
polish on whatever he was working on. As she
approached she remembered he had an appointment with Maurice Larosa, the antique
dealer. She paused, loath to interrupt a business
talk.

Their conversation drifted through the open
door, holding her riveted.

"She's a champion kid, Maurice," Jack declared with pride. "Sleeps through the night. No

worries at all. You'd better have a daughter next time.''

"I guess boys are noisier,'' came the rueful reply. "She's got your chin, Jack.''

"Chip off the old block. Though her eyes are just like Nina's.''

"The fair hair must come from you.''

"I guess so. She's going to be a stunner, Maurice. Blonde hair and big brown eyes.''

"Sounds like she's got you wrapped around her little finger already,'' Maurice remarked in amusement.

Jack laughed. "That's my daughter. You'd better warn your son not to mess with her. I'm riding shotgun on this kid.''

Nina couldn't help smiling. If there had still been any question about Jack's attitude towards Charlotte, it was more than answered by the doting expressions she was hearing.

"Well, I must be going,'' Maurice said, dragging his mind back to business. "Great job on the desk, Jack. My client will be delighted with it.''

"I'll get Gary to deliver it this afternoon. I'll show you out through the workshop, Maurice. Something else I want you to see.''

Self-conscious about eavesdropping, Nina moved beyond their sight as the two men started out of the room. "Mind Charlotte, Spike,'' Jack called over his shoulder. "Won't be long.''

This cavalier instruction to his dog piqued Nina's curiosity. As soon as the coast was clear she returned to the doorway into the rumpus room. Spike was sitting on his haunches beside the capsule, cocking his head attentively as Charlotte waved her fists and burbled. An inquiring whine came from his throat. Charlotte raised her voice in a peremptory manner. Spike squatted down, dropping his head over the side of the capsule. Charlotte crooned at him.

Nina had the weird feeling Charlotte had this huge, intimidating animal wrapped around her little finger, too. Certainly she wasn't the least bit frightened of the dog. She grabbed a fistful of shaggy hair. Spike's huge lolloping tongue came out and gently swatted her chin. Charlotte crowed in delight. Having sensed Nina's presence, Spike turned his head and gave her a look as if to say, "Well, she asked for it."

"That's fine, as long as you don't eat her," Nina heard herself say indulgently, and wondered if she had taken leave of all common sense. But the dog settled down contentedly and let Charlotte play with his hair, not so much as twitching an ear as the baby cooed her pleasure, obviously thinking it a great game.

"Don't worry. Spike thinks he's her stand-in mum."

She half-jumped as Jack's arms slid around her waist then relaxed as he gently pulled her against him.

"He's such a big dog." She sighed.

"All the better to keep her safe. Spike would lay his life on the line for her, Nina. But if you want a smaller dog for her..."

"No." It was obvious that dog and baby had bonded in some perfectly natural way that both were comfortable with. Jack undoubtedly had something to do with it, and she trusted his judgment. "I suspect you're losing your dog to Charlotte," she warned good-humouredly.

"Mmm." He nibbled her ear. "There's something very seductive about little beings, babies and pups and kittens and chicks. I think this might be the first time Spike's been in at the beginning, and he's not going to miss out on knowing how things develop."

She knew intuitively Jack was really speaking for himself. He didn't want to miss out on anything, either. Next time he would be with her throughout her pregnancy. There would be nothing lonely about it. Nothing lonely at all.

"The nurse said I've healed very well," she informed him. "And quickly, thanks to you taking every possible strain off me. I can get back to work now."

His head lifted. She felt his chest expand, and a long breath wavered through her hair. "Nina, the boys have been making you the perfect table to suit your working needs. We could turn the sunroom into a professional sewing room for you. It's only a fifteen-minute drive to Sally's for appointments."

"I must call Sally," she said, smiling over his plan.

"I'm sure she wouldn't mind."

Nina turned in his embrace to let him see the happiness and certainty glowing in her eyes. "I want to call her about a date for our wedding. If you still want to marry me."

"Want to..." He laughed, unable to contain his joy. "We're going to have all the frills Sally can think of."

"Her charges are high, Jack," she warned, laughing with him.

"Who cares? It'll be the best day of our lives. Charlotte can be a flower baby."

She arched an eyebrow. "Maybe we should have a flower dog, as well."

He shook his head, his eyes adoring her. "I love you, Nina Brady."

She looked at him with all the brimming emotion in her heart, this incredibly caring man, her lover, her partner in life, the father of her future family. "I love you, Jack Gulliver," she answered with vibrant passion, and went up on tiptoe to kiss him.

It was a kiss of promise, of absolute commitment, but most of all, of love and trust and deep pleasure in their togetherness. It was the beginning of the song of belonging.

CHAPTER NINETEEN

JACK slowly surfaced from deep sleep, feeling decidedly groggy. He recollected it had been a big night, a superb dinner and lots of champagne, he and Nina celebrating with Sally, riding a high from the great spread Nina had been given in a bride magazine, beautiful photographs of her best designs. Then he realised what had woken him. The kid was yelling.

He struggled out of bed, trying not to disturb Nina, who hadn't budged. Big night. A well-deserved big night. He didn't want the kid waking her up and spoiling sweet dreams of success and recognition of her talent. She'd worked hard for it. A special night for her.

Everything had been peaceful when they'd arrived home. Ben, who'd volunteered to baby-sit, had assured them there'd been no problems. The kid was six months old now. Shouldn't be yelling at this hour. Jack frowned at the numbers illuminated on the bedside clock radio. Four-seventeen.

The night-light in the hall gave a dim glow, guiding him out of the bedroom. He frowned as he saw a brighter light coming from the kid's bedroom. Someone must have left the touch-lamp on. The yelling stopped, but Jack kept going, deciding he might as well see if something was wrong. Switch the lamp off, as well.

He reached the doorway and halted in his tracks. His three-year-old daughter, along with her ever-faithful friend and companion, Spike, were lined up beside the cot, eyeballing the baby. Charlotte planted her hands on her hips and held forth to her little brother.

"Listen up, kid! You and I need to come to a 'commodation. I don't like being woke when it's still dark. Spike doesn't, neither."

Spike dutifully whined his displeasure.

"Now I'm going to teach you what's what." She stepped over to the lamp and tapped it until it went off. "This is dark. Have you got that, kid? Dark," she repeated for good measure. "You keep quiet when it's dark."

A raspberry from the cot.

The lamp came on again. "This is light. You can start yelling when it's light—" she wagged an authoritative finger at the baby "—but not before. And don't blow raspberries at me. Show some respeck. This is your big sister talking."

A becoming silence from the cot.

"That's better," Charlotte declared with satisfaction. "You've got to be a fast learner in this family, kid. Give him a lick for being a good boy, Spike."

Spike's tongue reached through the slats of the cot and swatted Patrick's hand.

"Right! Now I'm going to give you dark, and Spike and I are going back to bed. You might as well go to sleep again. You can wake up when it's light.''

The lamp went off. Jack scooted to his bedroom before the education brigade marched into the hall and to their bedroom. He listened for a while to make sure everything was all right. Silence reigned. He slid into bed and lay there with a huge grin on his face. Charlotte was definitely a champion kid.

Nina rolled against him and snuggled, sleepily mumbling, "Love you."

"Love you, too," he murmured, kissing her forehead.

He had a great wife, a smart daughter, a fast-learning son, an obliging dog.

What more could a man want?

Maybe another kid. When and if Nina felt up to it. After all, Patrick needed a younger brother or sister to pass the family lore onto. Fatherhood, Jack decided, was addictive. Especially with a family like his. On that contented thought, he closed his eyes and went back to sleep, serene in the knowledge all was well with his world.

If you are looking for more titles by

EMMA DARCY

Don't miss these fabulous stories by one of
Harlequin's most renowned authors:

Harlequin Presents®

#11604	THE SHEIKH'S REVENGE	$2.99	☐
#11632	THE SHINING OF LOVE	$2.99	☐
#11659	A WEDDING TO REMEMBER	$2.99 U.S.	☐
		$3.50 CAN.	☐
#11745	THE FATHERHOOD AFFAIR	$3.25 U.S.	☐
		$3.75 CAN.	☐
#11833	THE FATHER OF HER CHILD	$3.50 U.S.	☐
		$3.99 CAN.	☐
#11848	THEIR WEDDING DAY	$3.50 U.S.	☐
		$3.99 CAN.	☐

(limited quantities available on certain titles)

TOTAL AMOUNT	$
POSTAGE & HANDLING	$
($1.00 for one book, 50¢ for each additional)	
APPLICABLE TAXES*	$_____
TOTAL PAYABLE	$_____

(check or money order—please do not send cash)

To order, complete this form and send it, along with a check or money order
for the total above, payable to Harlequin Books, to: **In the U.S.:** 3010 Walden
Avenue, P.O. Box 9047, Buffalo, NY 14269-9047; **In Canada:** P.O. Box 613,
Fort Erie, Ontario, L2A 5X3.

Name: _____

Address: _____ City: _____

State/Prov.: _____ Zip/Postal Code: _____

*New York residents remit applicable sales taxes.
 Canadian residents remit applicable GST and provincial taxes.   HEDBACK6

⬦HARLEQUIN®
®

Look us up on-line at: http://www.romance.net

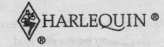